TALES
OF THE AMBER RING

Told by Miloš Malý
Illustrated by Petr Sís
Translated by Vladimír Vařecha

ORBIS PUBLISHING · LONDON

© Artia, Prague 1981
First English edition translated from the Czech
and published in Great Britain by
Orbis Publishing, London 1985
Graphic design by Sylvie Mikulcová

ISBN: 0-85613-531-3

Printed in Czechoslovakia by Svoboda, Prague
1/01/38/51-01

CONTENTS

The Bird
and the Amber Ring

There is hardly anyone left today who will remember how many kingdoms the Earth was divided into in those fairy-tale times. However, I do know of one which was absolutely different from any of the others.

It lay far in the north in the region of birch forests and groves, in the land of wide meadows where the wind raced wildly, driving the icy waves of the sea to spill over the shores.

It was a kingdom abounding in both game and birds. The people who lived there fished, herded cattle and sheep, and tilled the fields. Like every other country it had its rich and poor, and good men as well as some bad ones. And there was a king reigning over the land, so you might wonder what the people lacked.

Well, what they lacked were fairy tales to be recounted in the little cottages on winter evenings when blizzards raged behind the windows, or in the fields by a smoky fire, or during festivities in the castle hall.

Those fairy tales were said to have been carried away by Bulbulis, the magic bird, who had disappeared one day and never been seen again. In vain seafaring men on their voyages to distant shores inquired about the bird, in vain the king sent out brave and gallant knights in search of him.

At last one day a frail old man came limping to the castle gate, and insisted on seeing the king about a matter of supreme importance.

"He must know where Bird Bulbulis is, for what could be more important than that?" said the sentry to himself, so he took the visitor to see the king.

The sad monarch was slumped on the throne, surrounded by ten castle scribes with quill pens steeped in ink, and very long parchments before them, and a single sentence was written on each of the parchments:

"Once upon a time there was a king who did not know where Bird Bulbulis had gone."

The old man looked at each parchment, shook his white head, and humbly stood in the corner waiting to hear the king go on dictating to his scribes.

But he waited in vain. After a whole hour of silence the king struck the table with his sceptre, and said, "I have forgotten how it goes on, or else it is a bad fairy tale. Come again tomorrow, I hope to think up something better..."

Only after the scribes had gone did the old man step out of the corner, but then he boldly approached the throne, and said, "No, you won't think up anything better, because Bulbulis has carried all the fairy tales away, as you know very well."

The king was taken aback by the old man's sudden appearance, but the agreed sadly, saying, "I know, but what am I to do, when there is no one who can give me advice?"

"I will advise you. Listen carefully," said the old man. "Bird Bulbulis goes to sleep in a golden cage which hangs on the three-topped linden tree. That linden tree grows in the garden near a royal palace, and the palace lies behind nine meadows, nine hills, and nine rivers. But remember, only one of pure and good heart will know how to deal with Bulbulis."

"Then who am I to send to fetch him?" asked the king, but there was no reply. Where the old man had stood there was only an empty spot before the throne!

"Either this was all only a dream," murmured the king, "or . . . or he was a real fairy tale Old Man!"

For sheer joy he jumped off the throne, and quickly recited what he had been told. He was sure he had not forgotten anything; but now he had to decide whom to send to fetch the bird.

Nor did this seem such a great problem all of a sudden. "Do I not have three sons, all squarely built like birch trees?" The king struck his forehead, though it did occur to him that the youngest was rather stupid and would probably find it hard to come to terms with the world.

He pulled the bell. Once, twice, three times, and the princes appeared before him.

"I know now where the magic bird is hiding with our fairy tales," announced the king solemnly. "I should be happy if at least one of you would set out in search of him, and whichever of you succeeds in bringing him back shall succeed me on the throne."

Immediately all the three sons volunteered for the task. So the king decided that the eldest would be the first to set out to search for the magic bird behind nine meadows, nine hills and nine rivers.

So the eldest son picked a good steed, and girded himself. When his brothers were bidding him farewell, he made a notch with his sword on the castle gate, and said, "Come and look at the gate every morning. Should blood appear on the notch, then you will know I am in danger, and you must come to my rescue."

Then the eldest brother set out on his journey. Quickly he crossed the nine meadows, his horse easily climbed the nine hills and even managed to cross the nine rivers. And the moment he crossed the last of them he found himself in front of a royal palace with a big garden around it.

The prince dismounted, tied the black horse to a golden pillar and boldly stepped inside. He wandered about the magnificent empty halls, until he finally reached the King of that Ninth Country.

Without beating about the bush he said, "I have come to get Bulbulis, the magic bird who carried away all fairy tales from our kingdom. Do you know anything about him?"

"Of course, I do, my lad," said the King of the Ninth Country. "Bulbulis goes to sleep every evening in a golden cage which hangs on a three-topped linden tree in my own garden. However, I must warn you — many gallant heroes have come here before you, and none has ever carried Bird Bulbulis away. They all vanished, the earth seems to have swallowed them up."

The last words did not even reach the prince's ears. Evening was drawing near, and he was in a hurry to get to the garden to find the golden cage and lay his hands on the bird.

It was an enormous garden, but there were no flowers in it, and it was so thickly set with birch trees that the prince found it difficult to get through them. It was already dusk when he finally came to a little glade, and there at last he saw what he had been looking for, the three-topped linden tree. In the middle of the tree hung the golden cage with its door open.

Then the prince heard the song of birds, a song of such uncommon loveliness that he stood amazed. Suddenly the whole glade was lit up with a golden light, and before the prince had recovered from his bewilderment, Bird Bulbulis alighted on a branch next to the golden cage.

All the birds were suddenly hushed as if dazed with the golden beauty until Bird Bulbulis spoke in a sad voice:

"Everybody is asleep now, and there is not a living soul to tell me to go to sleep as well."

"Go to sleep, Bird Bulbulis, go to sleep," said the prince, as though compelled, and at that moment the bird struck him with his wing, and the prince turned into a birch.

The next morning, as they had done many times before, the two younger brothers came to inspect the notch in the gate, and lo and behold, there were drops of blood gushing out from it.

"I must be off at once," said the middle one, and having made another notch in the gate he bade the youngest, "Come every day, and if you see blood here as well, you must come to my rescue."

The middle brother reached the ninth country like his brother before him, found the three-topped linden tree in the garden, and when dusk fell Bulbulis appeared.

This time, too, the bird said in a sad voice, "Everybody is asleep now, and there is no one to send me to sleep as well."

However, the middle prince did not utter a sound. So Bulbulis made his moan even more heart-rending: "Is there really no one about to help me when I can't fall asleep?"

This time the young man could not contain himself, and he told Bulbulis to go to sleep. So he, too, was turned into a green birch by the bird.

Thus it happened that the following morning Ilin, the youngest prince, saw blood on the castle gate. He rushed to his father to give him the news and to tell him that he, too, must go out into the world.

The king was reluctant to let Ilin go. The youngest prince was no flower of wisdom; how could he bring Bulbulis back when the elder brothers had not?

But then he recalled what the old man said — he who wants to catch the bird must be a person of a good and kind heart. And as it was Ilin who was the most good-hearted of the three brothers, the king eventually agreed.

So the youngest prince rode on his white horse across nine meadows, over nine hills and across nine rivers till he reached the ninth kingdom. He was lucky to find the big garden and the golden cage in the midle crown of the linden tree.

And after a while the golden bird appeared. He sat on a branch beside the cage, and having looked round started his usual complaint: "Everybody is asleep now, only I am not. Who is going to help me with at least a word of encouragement?"

Ilin kept silent.

"Is there really not a living soul around?" Bulbulis said after a while. "How glad I should be to doze off."

Yet even this time the prince kept mute. The golden bird waited a while, but then he shrugged his wings and murmured, as if to himself,

"What can be done! I shall have to go to sleep by myself."

Not even then did Ilin betray his presence with a single word. Bulbulis jumped into the cage, hung down his head, and before long he was breathing so heavily his golden feathers were trembling.

This was exactly what Ilin had been waiting for. He crept close to the linden tree, and saw that the bird had an amber ring round one of his claws. He pulled it off gently, and shut the door of the cage. Suddenly, however, Bulbulis woke up.

"Let me out, let me out, or I will turn you into a birch!" he started shouting.

Ilin only laughed.

"I wouldn't let you out for the world. And if you make such threats, you are sure to have enchanted my brothers as well. Be quick to confess and tell me how to get my brothers back, or you shall know the power of my sword!" And he held his weapon in front of Bulbulis' golden beak.

Well, this was the right way to talk to the bird.

"Those two birches just in front of you are your two brothers," Bulbulis hastened to reply. "And to make them come to life again, you must throw a handful of earth at the roots."

Ilin did so, and that moment the two brothers embraced him joyfully, safe and well, just as they had been before. However, they were not the only ones whom the bird had deprived of human shape. All the birches in the garden had been his doing. And so they set free one young man after another till only one tree remained, and that was a genuine one.

There was so much pleasure and rejoicing. Even the King of the Ninth Kingdom came to the garden to have a look, and when he learnt what had happened, he had a great feast prepared in celebration.

When the rejoicing was over, everybody set out for home. And so did the three brothers. They were in no hurry, and even travelled as far as the sea into which the ninth river flowed.

Ilin carried the golden cage with Bulbulis inside, and did not notice that his brothers were gazing at it with envy every now and then. Instead of being grateful, they were pondering how they might get hold of the golden bird themselves. And envy being the worst of sins, they agreed to do away with Ilin.

When they lay down on the seashore that evening, the two pretended to go to sleep. And the moment the youngest brother had fallen asleep they bound him hand and foot, and threw him as far as they could into the sea. Afterwards they took the cage with Bulbulis in it, and rode home without even looking back.

Ilin did not drown, however. Not far from the spot where his brothers had cast him was the amber castle of the Queen of the Seas. She was well aware of what had happened, and at once sent her serving men to bring the prince to the castle, whereupon she herself breathed a breath of life into him once again.

When Ilin came to, he could not believe his eyes: the walls of the chamber where he found himself were inlaid with conches and seashells, the chandeliers were set with enormous pearls, the rich carpets had been woven out of tender green seaweed, and at his bedside sat the Queen of the Seas, whose face was of such unspeakable beauty that it took his breath away.

"Am I dead?" asked the prince in astonishment.

"You are in my amber castle to which you have been brought by the fairies," smiled the Queen of the Seas. "I know you have a good heart, that is why I did not allow you to die."

"But my brothers took Bird Bulbulis away from me, so now I am not going to hear a single one of the fairy tales the bird carried away from our kingdom," said the prince with sadness in his heart, though he had been saved.

But the queen shook her head.

"You shall hear them, Ilin. The fairy tales are hidden in the ring which you took off the bird's foot. It is enough to put the ring on your finger and turn it nine times. Without the ring not even Bulbulis knows any fairy tales."

"Doesn't he?" asked Ilin. The queen shook her head and he put the ring on his finger, and started to turn it round slowly.

After the ninth turn birds' songs were heard coming from above, just like the ones that had sounded when Bird Bulbulis had come flying into the garden. Then Ilin heard a quiet voice. The bird had begun, once again, to tell his stories.

The Ash Tree

No sooner had winter passed, and the sun driven the last traces of snow away into the dark corners of the forest, than snowdrops and oxlips blossomed forth in the meadows, and the air sounded with birds' cries. All nature fell head over heels into preparations for the great spring festival.

The first trees to turn green on the bank of the brook were the willows and sallows, then the white-barked birches put on their festive garments and stood in the grove like virginal bridesmaids, ready to dance.

The old spreading oak took it easy, pondering what would suit him best. Eventually, he had a suit made of large, indented leaves, which was indeed a perfect fit.

Only the ash tree slept on and on. He did not hear the buzzing of the bees or the cries of the birds; not even a spring thunderstorm was enough to wake him. But in the end, a strong wind shook him soundly and woke him up.

The ash tree looked round him, and saw the other trees all clad in green, so he said, "Spring has come, has it?"

"A long, long time since, and you keep on sleeping," laughed the birches, and the wind carried that laughter all over the forest.

So the ash tree asked no further questions. Instead, he quickly set about making his suit so as not to be a laughing stock. But as the old saying goes: haste makes waste, and the ash tree soon began to realize this. His leaves were neither big nor nicely patterned. All he managed to bring forth was a meagre amount of small leaves, set at all angles, sawlike and rugged, hardly enough to cover his nakedness. So once again he was derided by the other trees, and he was unhappy with his own work. However, he most solemnly resolved not to be the last to put his leaves away when autumn came.

And so, no sooner had the summer passed, and the first cold north wind blown than he asked, "Has autumn come yet?"

"Yes, it is coming, it is coming," answered the trees with a soft rustling of their leaves, all sorry and sad at the thought that they would have to part for a time with all their magnificence.

But the ash tree was delighted. He threw away his ill-fitting suit, and so once again he stood in the forest like a ragamuffin, while the other trees fought the north wind for a long time to save each single leaf.

Do you think the ash tree learned a lesson from this for the following year? Far from it. He never remembered anything, and came to the same sorry end as before, and it has been the same with him in that Land of Amber ever since. In spring he is the last to put on his dress, and in autumn he is the first to drop his leafy garment.

The Woodcutter, the Devil and the Princess

One day a young woodcutter — his name was Steps I believe — was trying to fell a gigantic beech in a deep forest. Suddenly, before him appeared a beautiful marten in a lustrous fur coat, with eyes like beads, who curiously examined him. The woodcutter threw a branch at her, but she skipped aside and in a moment sat down on a stump as if to see what he was going to do next. Steps shambled casually to the stump, and swooped. But the marten shot out like lightning and peeped at him from behind a birch, as if to say, "Well, come on! Catch me if you can!"

The woodcutter got angry and jumped after her, but he was no match for the swift, wild animal. There she was, peeping at him cheekily from behind a small bush. And the chase went on: the marten on the little rock, the woodcutter after her; the marten across the brook, Steps hopped — and there he was after her on the other bank. He nearly caught her by the tail, but one dashing move and she was gone!

All day long the man went after the marten in unrelenting pursuit. She led him into the depth of the primeval forest, and in the end vanished completely, as darkness fell.

The woodcutter looked sullenly around — he did not know these parts, he had never been here before. With night upon him, he would hardly find his way home now. He would be sure to get lost.

I will stay here overnight and in the morning I'll get out of here one way or another, Steps said to himself, and climbed up into a spreading oak. He made himself at home on a bushy branch, tying himself to it lest he should tumble down in his sleep right into a wolf's mouth, and was fast asleep before you could say Jack Robinson.

He did not sleep long, however. Before midnight he was awakened by a medley of voices. He listened for a while, adapting his eyes to the darkness, and saw that on the little clearing under the oak various animals were quarrelling, one trying to shout down the other. In their midst lay the dead forester dressed in his gala uniform with gold buttons, and the animals were arguing about which of them was going to sing the dirge over his grave.

The greyhound growled that he was the dead man's most faithful friend, how many times he had followed him about the forest, always faithfully to his heel, how he had beaten up game for him when they were hunting together, and how, on more than one occasion, he had taken his master home from the inn.

The cat, in her coaxing voice, referred to her intimate friendship with the forester's wife. Many were the times the two of them had washed and tidied up the whole of the forester's house!

The bear grumbled hoarsely that it was he, Misha, whom the forester had always consulted like his own brother whenever there was something new to be undertaken in the woods, and he, the strongest of all animals, was going to sing the dirge over the dead man's grave. And did they not all know the bear's mighty bass?

The eagle, for his part, maintained that he, the King of the Air, would best sing the dirge up in the heights. Anyway, the forester had never watched anyone with so much delight as he watched the eagle as he glided on his wings below the clouds!

The ant, that multi-legged miniature creature, was yelling till his voice nearly gave out: the dead man loved him most, since he was industrious by nature and could put away all the pine-needles in the forest on one heap.

The sparrow, with his cheek, cut the ant short, and claimed the forester had been exceedingly fond of him as well; he had never chased him away from the courtyard when he was sharing a grain or two with the hens.

"Who dares to talk about the courtyard?" the vain cock intervened. "There I myself have been sovereign lord from time immemorial. No one has such a beautiful and piercing voice as I have. Just look at my lovely blue, red and violet feathers! And does not the nose of our dear departed sport the same colours? Do you see the likeness? To be sure, I am his nearest relative. So it is only right that I should sing the solemn dirge for him!"

Now this set off a real row among the animals, all of them shouting at once.

Just at that moment the woodcutter jumped off his branch into the disorderly cluster of quarrelling beasts. He made the following proposal: "You are right, each one of you, but the trouble is that one of you has a voice which is weak, the other's voice is very strong, the third too high, the fourth awfully deep again. And if you were to sing all together, believe me it would sound simply terrible. With your permission I will sing the dirge for the forester on behalf of you all. I happen to be a chorister, and can sing quite a few lovely dirges."

The animals agreed. Indeed, they were happy the woodcutter could settle their quarrel so wisely.

Thus their beloved forester had a decent burial, and over his grave Steps sang a very sad dirge in seven verses in his soft, sweet voice.

The animals were deeply moved, and the burial over, they thanked the singer for having sung with so much feeling. As they bid him farewell, they promised they would help him, too, in time of need. He just had to think of any one of them, should he ever find himself in a spot, and he would change into that animal. Steps thanked the kind animals, and set out for home across the forest.

I don't know why I should ever want to change into a bear or an ant, he said to himself with a smile, on recalling what the animals had offered him, but he liked their being so grateful.

For a long time he walked through the woods, until he thought he must have lost his way again, when he encountered a very sad young fellow. No sooner had Steps addressed him than the young man burst into tears and told the woodcutter the story of his misfortune:

"Years ago there was a hunt in these very woods, and the king lost his way. He wandered about one day, then another day, and it was only the third day that he met a man with shaggy hair who limped because he had a hoof on his left foot. This was Lucifer, who offered himself to the king as a guide, promising he would lead him out of the forest, but for a price. He would come to the royal herd every day to choose one pig, and when he had taken away the last, the king would have to give him his daughter, Princess Daisy.

"The king vacillated, but then he remembered that his herd had as many pigs as there are clouds, so many that he could hardly manage to count them. Thus this hell's master would have to come and fetch pigs for many years, before he walked away with the last. And by that time the little princess would have grown into a woman, and would long have been married and gone to some faraway land. So the king gave the Devil his word with a light heart, and Lucifer at once guided him out of the thick forest straight to the castle gate.

"It was not long before the king, preoccupied with his cares, forgot all about the meeting in the deep forest. But the Devil did not forget. Evening after evening he visited the royal herd to pick the fattest pig, and dashed away with it to hell.

"Several years passed, and the king's herd had thinned until there were but a few weak and lean little pigs left. At that time the king recalled his agreement with the Devil, and his mind became troubled. Dismissing the old swineherd, he engaged a young one. He paid him well for protecting what was left of the herd, but it was all in vain. Every day one pig was gone. Now all that remained of the whole herd were three little sucking-pigs. The king wanted to put the swineherd in prison, but the young man fled, and the king was utterly at a loss. Just three more days, and the herd would be gone. Afterwards, the Devil would come to take away the princess. The king was now looking for a brave man, and promising half of his kingdom to him if he saved the princess."

"Take me to the king at once," said the woodcutter. "I will try to do away with the Devil."

The young man tried to talk him out of it, but in vain. So they set out, and towards evening reached the royal castle. Steps immediately offered himself to the king as his swineherd.

"All there is left of my herds are the last three little pigs, but it is on them that the life of my beloved daughter depends," said the king sadly. "If you succeed in preserving them, I will give you half of my kingdom. If not, you shall be thrown down into the dungeon."

The woodcutter thought for a while, but a moment later Princess Daisy came in to look at the brave young man. When Steps saw her gracious beauty he was resolved. He bowed to the princess, then to her father, and said, "Your Majesty, I don't want half of your kingdom. But if I overcome Lucifer, you will give me the princess for my wife."

The king was furious at the young man's audacity, and said he would not give the princess in marriage to a woodcutter. Steps rejoined by insisting he would accept no other reward. This was something that greatly took the fair princess's fancy, and she gave the young man a secret smile. So what was the king to do? Either he would marry his daughter to the gallant woodcutter, or else in three days the Devil would take her away. So the king relented, and the new herd went off to the sty to stand guard over the last three sucking-pigs. One of these could now hardly stand on its little legs, and was dead by the evening. As Steps was burying it under the apple-tree, there was a swishing movement over his head, and before he recovered from his surprise, the Devil seized one pig, and the next moment a sulphurous smell was all that he left behind.

"Dear me," cried the astonished young man. "Now I will really have to be on my guard, for there is only the last little pig left."

The next day Steps was careful not to let the last little pig out of his sight. Nevertheless, in the afternoon, as the swineherd was leaning over the fountain to put some water in his jug, the Devil flew in rapidly, grabbed the little pig, and vanished again with it in his claws.

The woodcutter was dumbfounded. So tomorrow the Hell's disciple would come to fetch Princess Daisy, and he himself would be thrown into the dungeon. Then he remembered the animals and the promise they had given him. At once he changed into a greyhound, and set out chasing the Devil on his sulphurous track. Before long he caught up with him and said, "In Hell you've got pork for dinner every day, haven't you? And don't you get fed up with it?"

"Why, of course," admitted the Devil. "I can't bear the sight of pork any more nowadays."

"I know of something better," suggested the greyhound. "Beyond eight forests a terrible robber is just being hanged. Hurry up, that would be something for you."

The Devil dropped the pig, and off he flew beyond the eight forests. He looked for the gallows, inquired about the robber, but could find nothing.

"I have been deceived. Well, just wait till tomorrow!" threatened the Devil.

Meanwhile, the greyhound changed into Steps again, and he brought the last pig into the pen, fed and washed it, and took it to bed with him.

The next day, the swineherd did not budge from the sucking-pig, constantly guarding it like the apple of his eye. In the evening, however, as he bent down to pluck a few nettles to put into its feed, he heard a fluttering sound over his head, and then all he saw was the Devil taking the piglet off to Hell with him. Quickly Steps changed into an eagle, caught up with the Devil a while later, and mocked him:

"You, Devil, I thought you were carrying off a proper pig for yourself as usual, but I can see you have chosen a miserable weakling."

"You are right, eagle, it is the last little remnant of the king's herd. There was nothing to choose from any more," confessed the Devil sadly.

"I know of something better," said the eagle. "In the other world near a lake, a stepmother is beating an orphan, and may even be about to drown him. Go and fetch that evil female, that will be a good thing for you!"

The Devil thanked him, let go of the pig, and set out for the other world. There he looked all around, but could not find any stepmother or orphan, or even the lake.

"Once again the new swineherd has deceived me," fumed the Devil. "Just wait, tomorrow I will show him what's what."

In the meantime, the eagle had brought the little pig back into the sty. There he changed into a man again, gave the pig water to drink, fed it, washed it, and both went to sleep.

In vain did the woodcutter wait for the Devil on the third day. The evening had nearly come, and the Devil did not appear. It was shortly before midnight that the Devil appeared in the pen. He was looking for the last little pig, but that was well hidden in the straw. Steps changed into a cock and crowed three times. The Devil knew that his hour had struck. He jumped out of the pen, and flew over the ramparts of the royal castle. But as he flew past, he saw that the window in the princess's bedroom was left open.

Overjoyed, he flew in, seized the sleeping Daisy, and prepared to carry her off to Hell. Well he knew that he would again be duped by the clever swineherd, that it would probably be no good trying to wangle the last little pig out of him.

The woodcutter saw everything, and ran after the Devil as fast as his legs would carry him. He was anxious to get to know the road to Hell.

The Devil flew to a great rock, and there he suddenly disappeared in a tiny narrow chink. Steps put his nose on the hole — yes, it smelled strongly of sulphur.

This is the road to Hell, he said to himself joyfully, and changed into an ant.

The ant let himself down the crevice, creeping lower and lower until he found himself in absolute darkness. The way under the earth took a long time; suddenly the crevice ended, and the ant fell down through the darkness until he landed upon a silvery meadow where only the moon was shining. In the distance, at the end of the meadow, stood a magnificent crystal palace. So that was where Hell's master had taken the princess. But how was Steps to get into the palace? Before the ant could crawl from one end to the other, the princess might come to some misfortune in the palace.

So the woodcutter quickly changed into a sparrow, and there he was flying across the meadow, and then straight through the open window into the chamber where Daisy sat in a gilt armchair, all in tears.

The sparrow turned into the woodcutter again, and the princess rejoiced to see the smiling swain by her side. However, before they could exchange a word, Hell's master appeared, and was at Steps's throat. But the latter immediately turned into a bear, took the Devil into his shaggy arms, and squeezed him so hard that all the bones in his body crackled, and Lucifer gave up his infernal soul.

When Steps had changed from a bear into a man again, the princess embraced him and thanked him heartily for having delivered her from the Devil's power.

"We haven't won through yet, fair princess," said the woodcutter. "Now we must get back to Earth. The chink through which I dropped down here as an ant is so narrow that neither you nor I can get through."

The princess grew rather sad, but Steps did not give up hope and wandered round the crystal palace looking for some secret corridor that might lead back to the Earth. In the lowest cellar he discovered an oak chest, and in it lay a big book of magic. Steps dusted it and carefully turned its leaves. After a while he found what he was looking for. On the last parchment leaf he read the following advice:

"If you wish to get out from this underground realm back to the world, you must get possession of the diamond egg which is deposited in the raven's nest right at the very top of the ancient pine. The tree rises above the lake in the palace garden. You must succeed in passing with the diamond egg through the crystal gate, before you find yourself on Earth again. If you smash the egg against the Devil's rock this magnificent crystal palace will be transferred into the world along with you. But you must take care. The crystal gate is guarded by a wicked watchdog of a gate-keeper who loves nobody and hates cats in particular."

"This suits us admirably," rejoiced Steps, and at once changed into a cat. The little cat found the lake and the ancient pine, and climbed up to its very top, where the diamond egg lay in the raven's nest. With great care she took it into her mouth, holding it with her rough little tongue, then jumped down from the tree, and made straight for the crystal gate. Softly she stole into the gate-house where the wicked gate-keeper was having a nap in his armchair.

The cat rubbed herself against the gate-keeper's legs for a while, then she jumped onto his lap, and, purring happily, pressed herself against him. Suddenly the gate-keeper woke up and saw the cat on his lap. He nearly had a stroke. He grabbed the affectionate little beast by the tail, whirled it round furiously and flung it high up above the clouds.

The cat flew through the crystal gate and landed softly next to the rock which the Devil had used to enter Hell. At that very moment the cat changed into the woodcutter again and the man smashed the diamond egg against the rock till it burst into thousands of bits.

Instantly the crystal palace stood there, and the delighted Princess Daisy was running to meet Steps.

There was a glorious wedding and Steps invited all animals whose help had made his happiness possible. And the animals — first one after the other and then all together — sang a merry wedding song for the newly-weds.

The King
of the Misty Mountain

I don't know what the custom is in your part of the world, but in the region of Järven people have, from time immemorial, driven their horses to the pasture to graze after work every evening. Thus it happened that on one particular evening children were grazing all the village horses on the meadow near the forest below the Misty Mountain.

As usual, they made a little fire to bake some apples in the ashes and to cheer them up when the dark night descended on them. At first, they scampered round the fire, but later they sat close together and told terrifying tales about devils and werewolves, and especially about the Misty Mountain surrounded by magic charms, where no one has ever dared to tread, and which is constantly shrouded in impenetrable mist.

Talk was smoothly unfolding like the thread on a spindle, the apples were already giving off sweet scent, but the fire was dying down, and unless it was fed with a few loose sticks it would completely go out. But nobody felt like venturing into the dark forest.

As usual, the lot finally fell on Tiu. The others bade her fetch a few dry sticks. Tiu was the youngest of them all, and rather afraid of the forest. However, since she had no father or mother, everyone ordered her about and she was used to obeying them all.

So she went into the forest, but there was no brushwood to be found in the dark. She stumbled from one tree to another, and when she looked back after a while she could no longer see the fire, nor hear the voices of her playmates.

She called, burst into tears and called again, but the only answer she got was from the rustling trees in whose spreading tops the breeze was playing. Now and then Tiu heard the croaking cry of a bird; her cries had woken him up. Tiu was terrified by the noise, for she was still very young. Just as she was growing desperate, she saw a light in the distance. Rejoicing at having found her way back to her playmates after all, she wiped away a tear, bent down to pick up a dry stick against which she had stumbled, and in high spirits set out in the direction of the light.

After a while she reached a low hillock at the foot of which there was a blazing fire. She approached it gingerly, and saw a solemn-looking old man sitting there. He had a long silver-grey beard and was clad in a gorgeous garment trimmed with gold.

The old man gave her a friendly look, then beckoned to her and said in a kind voice, "Well, come, come, Tiu. I have been waiting for you. I heard you calling out in the forest. You have lost your way, haven't you? How kind of you to have brought me some wood for my fire. Well, throw it on the pile, and sit down beside me. You are chilled to the bone, and you must be hungry. Indeed, I have prepared a little bite for you just in case."

And the old man handed the child a silver dish full of strawberries and honey. The girl thanked him and fell to eating with great appetite, glancing now and then at the old man.

"I wonder if he is the King of the Misty Mountain himself?" she thought, and she guessed right, for he really was the magic king, kind and good to all people in need.

As though he could read the girl's thoughts, the old man gave three gentle knocks with his iron stick on the mountainside behind him. The mountain drew a little apart, and two little maidens came running out. Prattling merrily, they caught Tiu by the hands, and started dancing with her round the fire. Before long the three made friends and were playing together as if they had always known one another. They did not even notice how quickly the night passed.

When the sky was growing pink with the breaking dawn, the two little maidens ran back into the Misty Mountain. They returned after a while: one carried a basketful of sweet-smelling pastries, the other a big jug of warm milk. The king sat with the children around the stone table, and they all enjoyed their breakfast. Then he turned to Tiu, saying:

"It is good of you to have come to see my children of the Misty Mountain. They have not enjoyed such a fine game for a long time now. However, you must stay with us today to have some sleep. In a moment the bright day will be upon us and this is the time when we sleep here. But tomorrow, before the crack of dawn, if you like, the girls will show you how to get back to your village."

And so Tiu slept all day with her new companions in a magnificent chamber inside the Misty Mountain. But the moment the first star — the Evening Star — mounted the sky, all the three maidens once again engaged in playing and merry-making at the foot of the Mountain. What a marvellous time this was for Tiu. In her village no one had ever been so kind and gentle to her. Even so, she did feel homesick when the night was gone.

"I must be getting back now," she said to her companions, "my people will be afraid for my safety, and are bound to be looking for me now."

Before dawn broke, the girls again brought a basketful of good things and a jug of milk. They had breakfast, and after that came the moment of parting; all the girls were on the verge of tears. The old man tried to comfort them. He stroked Tiu's flaxen tresses, fixed a little silver buckle on to her dress, hung a little golden key round her neck.

Then he said, "Dear little girl, you have spent one day and two nights here with us. The time has flown like the wind, hasn't it? But meanwhile down there in the village seven long years have passed. When you go back home now nobody will know you any more. They forgot all about you long ago. Do not be afraid though, I have taken care of you. At the very end of the village there is now an orchard with a little cottage standing inside it. The cottage is yours. The key to it hangs round your neck. The orchard will bring you a lot of lovely fruit; you will sell it and make a good living. Only the pomegranate with the golden stem is one you must not sell. You must keep it for the man who will come and ask you to become his wife.

"Should you feel lonely and miss us, all you need to do is breathe three times on the silver buckle, and you will be with us again. You know we shall be pleased to see you any time.

"But you must not say a word to anyone about the Misty Mountain. If you ever gave away the secret, the whole spell would be broken. You could never again come back to stay with us, and I could never again help people in need.

"My daughters are now going to show you the way to your home. So, good luck, Tiu."

In tears, Tiu bade farewell to the kind old man, thanked him for his precious gifts, and set out for home with her companions. In a few moments they reached the edge of the forest, and Tiu saw her native village.

She kissed the sisters and promised to come and see them soon again. Then she walked along the path towards the village.

Here everything was changed beyond all recognition. In seven years both the village and the people had become different. Even Tiu herself had turned into a lovely maiden, straight as a birch-tree, a pleasure to behold! No one recognized her, nor did she recognize anybody. The former playmates of her childhood had turned into handsome young lads and graceful lasses.

At the end of the village in the middle of a large orchard stood the little cottage waiting for Tiu. She unlocked it with the golden key, stepped over the threshold, and began her new life.

Tiu was happy taking care of her fruit-trees. The pears, apples and plums that the orchard yielded were indeed splendid. People from far and near came to buy the amazing fruit, and they paid a good price.

One day a buyer brought his son with him, and the young man fell in love with Tiu and asked her to become his wife. She fell in love with him as well. She gave him the beautiful pomegranate with the golden stem which she had been keeping carefully, and a merry wedding-feast followed.

The young couple lived together in happiness and peace. When a little girl was born to them some time later, they were supremely happy. And thus another seven years passed.

However, Tiu found it impossible to forget the Misty Mountain and her friends living there. Often she remembered them while working, and on such occasions a dreamy sort of smile would spread over her face. Her husband often watched her, and never failed to ask, "What are you thinking about, Tiu? Why are you smiling like that? You are surely hiding something from me. Do tell me, please."

The young woman always started when caught by her husband in her reverie. But she knew she must not give away her secret. So she always made up some story just to allay her husband's curiosity.

One night, however, Tiu was seized with such a desire for the Misty Mountain that she could no longer resist it. She rose silently, so as not to wake her husband or her little daughter, dressed quickly, breathed three times on the silver buckle — and the magic worked. There was a soft breeze, and the next moment she found herself in the chambers of the Misty Mountain among her friends.

There was no end of joy and embracing and questioning, as they had not seen one another for seven years. Tiu told them about her lovely little daughter, and the maidens at once suggested she should bring her along next time she came.

"No, no, that can't be done," the old king warned them. "Do not bring your daughter here. She would have to stay here afterwards so that she might not betray the secret of the Misty Mountain to men. And you, Tiu, must be careful, for you know your husband suspects you."

Tiu got back home before daybreak and in silence she lay down in her bed again as if nothing had happened, and dreamed happy dreams about her secret friends. However, her husband had woken earlier that night to find his wife's bed empty. In vain did he look for her. He even went out into the orchard calling out to her, but it was as if she had been swallowed up by the sea. The whole night the poor man did not sleep a wink and he saw Tiu come quietly back at daybreak.

At breakfast in the morning he kept silent, and when he saw that mysterious blissful smile on his wife's face again, he asked her no questions and was exceedingly sad.

After a time Tiu was again overwhelmed by the desire to see her friends, and one night she set out for the Misty Mountain. Her husband watched everything, but said nothing in the morning, well aware that his wife would not tell him where she had gone.

When this happened a third time, the husband no longer knew what to do. So right after breakfast he went to see the village mayor and told him everything. The mayor was not a bad man, only a little indecisive; so he went to the rectory to tell the vicar. The vicar knew at once that there must be some magic behind it, so he went to consult the judge.

In the end they summoned the unfortunate Tiu to appear before the court, and questioned her as to where she, a married woman and mother of a little child, was spending whole nights.

Tiu kept silent. She did not know what to say in reply to that question. For she could not reveal her secret about the Misty Mountain. If she did, the gracious king would never again help any man in need!

When the young woman would not speak, they denounced her as a witch, and for those hell's associates there was but one punishment — burning at the stake.

So they called an executioner to come from the neighbouring town, and he and his henchmen built a stake on the common in front of the chapel, a high stake of pitchy logs. In the middle, the innocent Tiu was tied to a pole. She did not even cry any more. The only thing she could not understand was that her own husband did not stand up for her.

From far and near whole crowds of curious people gathered to watch the appalling sight.

When the judge gave the sign, the executioner fired the stake on three sides with pitchy wisps of straw, and the smoke and flames poured forth into the sky.

At that moment the whole place of execution became shrouded in impene-

trable mist, and when the wind had blown it away, the astonished crowd saw that the fire was out, the stake stood untouched, the pole in the middle was empty, and the young woman gone — she had just vanished!

The old king had carried her away to the Misty Mountain. Now Tiu could once again live there among her kind friends; however, every now and then sadness darkened her face. In those moments she thought of her little daughter.

"Do not be sad, Tiu," the wise king comforted her, "you'll see, when the time comes, everything will turn out all right again."

And so it happened. The little girl missed her mother badly. Often she would open Tiu's wardrobe, and breathe in the scent of her clothes, blissfully shutting her eyes, for she had the feeling her mother was quite near.

One day when she was alone at home she could not resist the temptation to dress in those clothes. As she was buttoning up the blouse, her hand struck against something hard.

"Look, what a lovely clasp! And it will be even finer when I have polished it up a bit," said the little girl to herself. She breathed on the clasp and polished it with her skirt. She breathed a second time and polished it till it shone like a mirror. Once again she breathed on the clasp. "Now it will shine like the sun," she thought, but at that moment a gentle breeze blew, and before she knew what had happened, she was standing in a magnificent chamber with her mother hugging her.

What more is there to tell?

Perhaps only so much as to say that they were all happy and contented now in the Misty Mountain. And what about the village?

There they found that the little daughter from the apple orchard had disappeared, but nobody except the father worried much about it. They concluded that she had been carried off by her mother, the witch, and forgot all about her.

However, the King of the Misty Mountain bore a grudge against the heartless people in the village. He found it unforgivable that out of sheer stupidity they had nearly put an innocent creature to death.

Therefore he denied moisture to their fields, meadows and gardens. So the corn in their fields dried up, the grass burnt by the sun's heat turned brown, the fruit was all worm-eaten and dropped to the ground.

Only the orchard which Tiu had cultivated was green, and wonderful fruit grew there all the time. It was a green island in the midst of a parched desert.

The mayor shook his head over the miracle. Judging by that, he said to himself, Tiu was in fact a good, just creature, and we, fools that we were, wanted to punish her with fire! That is why our own fields and meadows look as though they've been destroyed by a fire while her orchard has turned into a garden paradise!

In the end, let it be said in truth and justice that the mayor grew wise, though only after the event, and no one was ever tortured again in the region of Järven.

Why the Tomcat does not Wash till after Meals

The tomcat, as everyone knows, is an exceedingly tidy animal. Every now and then he wets his paw and takes great pains to improve the lustre of his fine fur coat. But have you noticed that cats will never wash until they have got through their meal? And do you know why?

Once upon a time — rather a long time ago — the big black tomcat got tired of eating nothing but mice. Suddenly, he felt like having more delicate fare. "The mouse never does anything but dig in the earth under the floor. She makes her nest in any dirty corner. How can she be expected to have tasty flesh?" Such were the gloomy thoughts revolving in the tomcat's round head. "If only I could catch a pretty young bird! He smells sweet with the breeze, the sun and the pines. That must be a tastier morsel!"

And so the tomcat sneaked along the ridge, and, after waiting a long time under a blossoming plum tree, he caught his prey, a lively tomtit, and carefully carried her off behind the cottage, where he hoped to feast in peace and quiet.

In the meantime, the tomtit had recovered from her initial shock, and she started a conversation with the tomcat.

"You are going to eat with those filthy paws of yours, are you? You sloppy beast! Don't you wash before meals?"

"I'm surprised at you. How can you feel like chirping such nonsense before you die?" growled the cruel black cat.

"Why, this is no nonsense! Haven't you ever noticed the farmer and the housewife?"

"How could I help doing so? I'm living with them!" the tomcat rejoined.

"And has it escaped your notice that people wash their hands before every meal?" asked the tomtit. "That they do not eat like pigs?"

"How dare you? I'm not a pig!" said the tomcat, deeply offended.

"So I hope you are going to wash those bedraggled paws of yours before you start eating," replied the tomtit.

"Oh, all right," murmured the tomcat gruffly. "Have it your own way. Everybody has his last wish granted."

He opened his mouth, and laid the tomtit into the grass; then he set about thoroughly licking his forepaws with his rough tongue.

The tomtit straightened out her crumpled wings, and having ruffled up her coloured feathers with her bill, she spread her wings — and was gone!

The tomcat jumped up with lightning speed — but too late. His claws just sawed through empty space. And from the top of a nearby birch the tomtit's merry note was heard.

"Took me in, that cunning little trickster! But it serves me right. I shouldn't try these newfangled ways at my age," spluttered the tomcat angrily. "I'll never again wash before feeding. I'll eat first, and afterwards improve my appearance." And that is what he has done ever since.

Luck and the Gold Duck

Once upon a time there were two brothers. Their father had carefully divided his property between them, and helped both his sons build new cottages. However, though both of them were equally diligent and hard-working, the younger one never came to terms with life. Whatever he tried went wrong. He sowed oats and they never came up, he went out fishing, and only just escaped getting drowned, and when he tried to keep a shop his only earnings were the debts he came home with.

Thus it went on from bad to worse, so in the end the poor man decided to take his life. He took a hemp rope, and set out for his brother's forest to find a suitable tree to hang himself on, for the trees in his own forest were so thin and stunted that no branch was strong enough to hold him.

The moment he found himself in the shadow of the forest he could not believe his eyes: All around there were big oaks, firs and pines falling to the ground, and when they fell they immediately turned into neat little piles of wood arranged into cubic metres, just waiting to be carted away. And strange to say, there wasn't a lumberjack in sight.

"Are you surprised?" he suddenly heard somebody say behind him. The poor man looked in that direction and in the bilberry growth he saw a dwarf, with a beard so long that it wound round his legs like a rug to keep him warm.

Before the young man could think of an answer, the dwarf ran his fingers gently through his beard till the hairs sounded like strings on a violin, and said, "All you can see here is my work. I am your brother's Luck. Luck fells the trees, Luck piles them, and sometimes even takes the wood to his courtyard."

"So that's how it is!" cried the poor man in spite of himself. "He has so much luck it even works for him, while I have never had good luck once in all my life, even to play with. There really seems to be nothing left for me but this rope..."

"You ought to be ashamed of yourself," said the dwarf. "You, too, have your own Luck, but you must be too lazy even to go out and look for it."

"So I am lazy, am I? Just tell me where I am to seek my luck, and I will gladly go to the very end of the world to find it." The younger brother lost his temper and threw the rope on the ground.

The dwarf only smiled.

"Your determination pleases me better than your lamentation, and that is why I will give you advice. You need not even go very far: At the end of your meadow is an old, half-dilapidated hayloft where you will find your Luck. He has slept there ever since you were born. Wake him up with a sound thrashing and he should work for you, just as I am labouring for your brother."

Having said this the dwarf seemed to dwindle into the bilberry growth, but the tune of his silvery beard was still to be heard among the falling trees.

The poor man did not tarry in the forest. He stalked off to the old hayloft, breaking off a hazel rod on the way.

Luck really was asleep in the hayloft. He was rosy-cheeked, beautifully round from doing nothing, and his beard was as long as that of the dwarf in the forest.

He did not seem to feel like waking up. Only after the younger brother had beaten him soundly with his hazel rod, he sat up, gave a yawn, and very much amazed asked:

"Why are you beating me? What have I done to you?"

"It is because you have not done anything, and are sleeping when you should be helping me," rejoined the poor man. "You are my Luck, aren't you?"

For a moment the fat dwarf surveyed him from top to toe and back again before he replied:

"You may be right, though I don't find you much to my taste. You look so worn out and decrepit that I am ashamed of you."

"Whose fault is that?" asked the man angrily. "Just wait and see what you are going to look like when I have given you a hiding with this rod." And once again he lifted his arm to strike.

The dwarf cried in terror:

"Why, what's the hurry? We shall come to terms yet, don't worry. Just go and place a net in the brook behind the cottage and before the week is out you shall be better off than your brother."

"How can I lay a net when I have no money to buy it with?"

Now this made the dwarf put on a sulky look. He said from the corner of his mouth:

"You do have some. Under the ground in the middle of your cottage you'll find five pennies. With these you can buy as many nets as you like. But mind my words — you had better never leave that cottage even if you get on very well. And now let me take a little nap, I have never been so exhausted in all my life."

Thereupon Luck closed his eyes, and before you could say Jack Robinson, he was asleep again. For a while the man stared at the dwarf snoring away happily, then he threw the rod away, and went to dig up the promised five pennies.

And there they were — at the first stroke of his hoe. So he bought a net and laid it that very evening near the bend behind the cottage. For the first time in their lives he and his wife and children went to bed without worrying about the morrow. "Even if my Luck does let me down I know where to find him, and I will teach him a proper lesson," he thought as he fell to sleep.

His Luck did not let him down, however. The next morning he found a duck in his net — the like of which the world had never seen. Each of her feathers was of pure gold, and before evening came she laid a big golden egg, for which the poor man's brother willingly gave him a hundred ducats on the spot.

As Luck had foretold, in a week's time the poor man became the richest man in the neighbourhood. He hired bricklayers to build him a new house, bought cattle, meadows, fields and forest, but the duck kept on laying golden eggs day in, day out.

Before long there was no one left in the neighbourhood rich enough to pay for the eggs. Nor did the younger brother feel like selling them cheap, or storing them at home. So he decided to try his luck with the golden eggs in the outside world. And having completely forgotten that his Luck had advised him never to leave home, he loaded his waggon with golden eggs, harnessed his horses, and went out over hill and dale into the wide world. Before leaving, he ordered his wife not to say a word about the golden duck to anyone.

Now let us leave the younger brother wandering about the world with his golden eggs, and recount what happened at home after his departure.

There were wonderful things indeed going on there. The news about the brother's wealth spread like wildfire all over the country, and many cunning fellows decided they would like to have the golden eggs in their own pockets. And they were especially interested in learning how such eggs were laid by the miraculous bird.

Thus it came to pass that various kinds of rogues, swindlers, cheats, snakes in the grass and other tricksters sought out the lonely wife in order to deceive her and cheat her out of the secret of the golden duck.

To begin with, the wife was on her guard, but when a general in golden epaulettes and with a long moustache appeared in the house, and courted her with greater perseverance than all the others, she took a fancy to him, and it was not long before she gave away the whole secret to him.

Of course, what the general was after was to get the golden duck for himself.

So he promised the wife he would take her to town where she would become his wife, would ride in a golden carriage, and receive the homage of everyone.

The peasant's wife listened, her eyes wide at the thought of these delights, yet she was still afraid of giving away her husband's property. In the end, however, the general persuaded her to show him the duck, saying he just wanted to have a look at her.

And that is what happened. The woman brought the golden bird from her hideout and the general, thrilled, began to inspect her feather by feather. Since each of them was of pure gold he had a good mind to tear off every feather, but the cotter's wife watched him like a hawk. In the end, he lifted the bird's wing, and was amazed to see the following inscription: WHOEVER EATS ME SHALL BE A KING.

He quickly dropped the wing again, but the peasant's wife could read and had instantly deciphered the inscription.

At once the two agreed they would kill the duck and roast her, but no sooner had the woman put the bird in the oven than they started quarrelling. The general wanted to be king alone, and the cotter's wife wanted to be queen alone. So they first shouted at each other, then they came to blows, chased each other around the courtyard, beat each other up, and in the heat of the quarrel forgot all about the duck.

But there was someone who did not forget: Michael, the son of the house, who was lying behind the stove and heard everything. When the duck was roasted, he pulled it out of the oven and ate it all up to the very last morsel.

After this, he did not tarry. He packed his bundle, and while the other two were still struggling in the courtyard, slipped out through the back gate, and then he set course direct for the royal city.

He had not even reached the end of the meadow, when, just in the spot where his daddy's Luck had been taking a nap, he came across a grey foal.

"My name is Serko, and I know you want to become king," he said in a human voice. "That's why I have come to help you. There is a flaming sword near my saddle, and I am so quick that no one ever catches up with me."

Michael thanked the steed, mounted him, girded himself with the flaming sword, and rode to the city.

It was no ride, it was a wild flight, and before the young man knew what happened they were passing through the city gate. It was only then that he noticed that the city walls as well as the houses were draped in black and the royal palace on the hilltop was all shrouded in the mourning crape.

So Michael asked the sentry at the gate, "Why are there black flags hanging all over the place? I hope it is not because the king has died."

"A much worse misfortune has befallen us, young man," the soldier waved his hand. "A terrible dragon has made his den in the cave under the castle. First he destroyed all the cattle, and then he took it into his head that he must get one maiden from the city every day. At that time a countryman arrived with a carriage full of golden eggs and brought us a temporary reprieve..."

"Well, that must have been my father!" the young man said.

"He has done a good deed," smiled the soldier. "When he saw what was going on here, he never asked a penny for his treasure, and personally went to feed the dragon with one golden egg a day. In recognition the king appointed him his first minister. But the trouble is that yesterday the store of eggs gave out, and today the dragon resolved that at midday our princess, lovely Catherine, must be given him to devour."

"And no one came forward to meet the dragon in armed combat?" said the young man in surprise.

"There were some," said the soldier sadly. "Knights and kings' sons came from every corner of the earth. In fact, the king promised that whoever overcomes the dragon shall receive the princess in marriage and succeed to the throne, but nobody ever got anywhere near the dragon. He killed all of them with his poisonous fumes."

Michael thanked the soldier for his words, bade farewell to him, and having ridden to a place where the sentry could no longer hear him, he asked his gentle steed, "Did you hear? Shall I go and fight the dragon?"

"Indeed, I am already taking you down to the cave," neighed Serko. "If you want to win and stay alive, you must remember not to take a single breath, or the dragon will kill you with his breath as he killed the others."

All that Michael had time to do was to nod in assent, for at that moment they were passing a procession of mourners among whom he recognized his father and also beheld the beautiful face of lovely Catherine. Though unhappy and in tears, she was lovelier than any maiden the young man had ever seen.

Then Serko found himself in front of the cave, and knocked against the rock with his hoof.

It was as if the dragon had been waiting for this. First, an enormous, monstrous crocodile head emerged with a gigantic cock's comb and eyes like watermelons, followed by a lizardlike body covered with sticky scales.

At the same time, Michael was covered in green poisonous fumes from the dragon's nostrils.

But the youth was ready. With bated breath he pulled his flaming sword out of its sheath, and wielding it with both hands, dealt the dragon such a blow that the monstrous head flew off.

Three new heads sprang up to replace the one. Yet Michael knew how to deal with those as well. All red in the face, he covered the dragon with blows, until the last head was rolling on the ground.

But even this was by no means the end of the fight. This time nine heads grew on the dragon's shoulders, and each of them pursued Michael, pouring forth poisonous vapours at him.

The youth knew he could not hold out much longer without taking breath, so he hacked at the monster with all his might till the sword made flaming circles in the air, and again there was one head after another tumbling down to the ground.

Now there remained only one — the ninth. Michael's strength was ebbing away, and if he was to deal the monster even one blow, he had to breathe in. At that moment he heard his gentle steed under him say:

"Do not breathe, Michael, just hold on to me so that you don't tumble down!"

And the horse kicked the last head with his hoofs till it broke into pieces.

This, however, was something the youth did not take in any more. He just held on to Serko's mane and there were red sparks dancing before his eyes.

At last the gentle steed allowed Michael to take breath. It was some time before he came to completely, but when he recovered, he found himself in the arms of his father, of fair Catherine and of the old king, being led in triumph to the palace.

And there a royal wedding was celebrated, with all due pomp and circumstance. There was eating, drinking, and feasting for a whole month, and then for a second and a third, and it was only at the end of the last day of that glorious wedding feast that Michael told his father what had happened at home, and how the golden duck had fared after he had left home.

For a while, the old man pondered, and then he said:

"Well, I ought to have listened to my Luck's behest even when he was sleepy, and should never have left home. I might have become a king myself. However, it is indeed better the way things have turned out: my only son is the ruler and has got the loveliest princess in the world. What I should like best of all is to be my son's minister. Let us leave those two in the cottage as they are — they can go on quarrelling about the roast till the house falls down on their heads."

Michael reigned as a wise king and rejoiced at having such a beautiful wife, his father made a good minister, while his father's wife still continued to fight with the general in the courtyard.

Well, and as to the old man's Luck, I heard it went right on sleeping in the old hayloft.

Every Cloud Has a Silver Lining

One day two old companions happened to meet at the market. They had not seen each other for a long time, and so they had plenty to talk about. As usual, the first topic was the weather.

"What bad weather we have been having, it keeps raining all the time," said the one.

But the other at once contradicted him: "I don't know what is bad about that. You should see my garden — what wonderful cabbage-heads have grown up there during these rains. They are as big as a man's head with a hat on!"

"That's fine. So in fact you have profited by bad weather," smiled the one.

But the other only sighed and said, "It might have been all right, only that devil of a goat has bitten off parts of each cabbage-head."

"Well, that's bad," admitted the first.

But the other only grinned and said, "Well, it was not so bad after all. I cut the goat's throat, pickled her and was about to smoke it."

"Well, that's the thing. So you and your family had a good time after all."

"Haha! Far from it, my dear!" frowned the fellow who had suffered the damage. "Just imagine, the rope that devil of a goat was hanging on suddenly broke after burning through, the meat dropped down into the fire, the embers burst, a fire broke out, and before I knew where I was, the whole smoking-chamber was burnt down."

The first man was startled. "Oh, that's a bad thing. That's really very bad!"

But the other quickly comforted him: "Don't you see? Why should it be so very bad! I had wanted to buy a new smoking-chamber, and a better one, for a long time, so I have it now."

"So the fire did some good after all!" said the first.

But the other only shook his head sadly. "Well, it would have been all right, but as I was putting the last beam into place, my wife appeared all of a sudden, the beam dropped on her head, and she lost the power of speech."

"Oh goodness, that is a terrible misfortune when a woman cannot speak!" started the first.

But the other just waved it off. "That would not have been such a terrible misfortune after all. But I called in a doctor, and he cured my wife before long."

"That's wonderful. I am so glad that it all turned out so well after all!" rejoiced the first. He was a good man and true, and worried by his friend's troubles.

"Far from it, just the opposite," rejoined the other. "My wife fell for the young doctor, left me and went to live with him."

"Well, that's a real piece of bad luck!" said his companion pityingly.

"Not at all bad luck!" smiled the other bitterly. "I pressed the doctor to the wall, and shook a whole potful of ducats out of him."

"God be praised, my friend, that everything has turned out all right in the end: you got rid of an unfaithful wife and now you have so much money that you don't have to do a spot of work as long as you live."

"How can it be all right! It turned out all wrong: I bought some more land, planted it with cabbage, toiled like a horse — and just look at the weather," complained the other.

"You are right," admitted the first. "Indeed, the weather has been bad again, it keeps on raining."

"I don't know what is bad about this. You ought to see what sort of cabbage have I grown during those rains. Yes, those are cabbage-heads as big as a man's head with a hat on!"

"That is fine. So in fact you have profited by the bad weather," laughed the first.

But the other only sighed and said, "It might have been all right, only that devil of a goat has bitten off all my cabbage-heads."

"Well, that is bad . . ." admitted the first . . .

And in this way the two friends go on telling each other how every cloud has a silver lining, and have no idea how to put an end to their never-ending conversation.

When you come to the market one day, you may still find them there. You should send them home, or their tea will get cold!

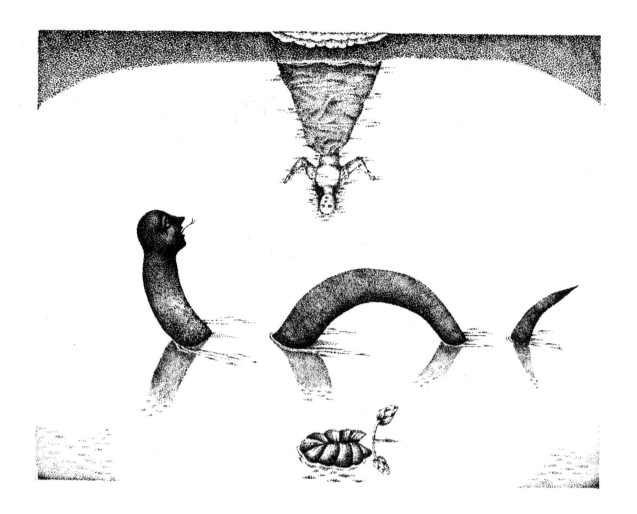

Egle

Once on a summer's day the three sisters from the manor farm went bathing in the lake. When they had tired of splashing about and frolicking in the water, they came out to put on their clothes again. Suddenly the youngest of them, whose name was Egle, gave a frightened cry. As she was reaching for her chemise, a big water-snake crawled out of the sleeve, and softly hissed at her.

"Go away, you monster!" cried the maiden when she recovered from her fright.

However, the snake would not be driven off. He settled firmly in the sleeve, and once again he hissed at the maiden, then spoke in a human voice: "Promise you will marry me, and I will let you have your chemise again." Egle stood transfixed with amazement. But her sisters burst out laughing: "He will make a fine bridegroom!" They dressed quickly, shouting merrily, "Make haste with the wedding, or we shall be gone and leave you here!"

What was the poor maiden to do? She could not go home naked. And her sisters were already leaving and throwing roguish looks at her.

So she said quickly, "Well, I will marry you." She said this as casually as she could, only to get back her chemise.

The moment the words were uttered the snake gave a contented hiss, and unwinding his body, slipped down into the lake.

Egle dressed quickly, and forgetting all about the snake, hurried home to catch up with her sisters. The next day as she was embroidering a festive table-cloth in her room, she suddenly heard a strange rustling sound, soughing and clapping like raindrops falling on stones. But outside the sun was shining like a golden ducat!

She looked out of the window — and could not believe her eyes!

The whole courtyard was full of all sorts of snakes, adders, slow-worms and other reptiles, one crawling over the other, the front ones already slipping up the staircase, and at the back behind the gate whole streams of others surging forward.

However, by then the first reptiles had already invaded the living-room, and the three fattest of them slithered right in front of the astounded husbandman. One of them gave a hoarse hiss, and said, "Farmer, we are the best men sent by the King of the Lake who wishes you to give him your youngest daughter in marriage."

"But that's impossible!" said the farmer stupefied.

"Why should it not be possible? Indeed, your daughter herself vowed to our king by the lake yesterday to become his wife."

"Well, if that is so, then nothing can be done about it," sighed the farmer and giving a sly wink to his wife said, "Don't cry, my dear. A promise is a promise. One day our little daughter would have married anyway, and she certainly would not marry a king. So why should we moan? Go and bring our dear little daughter — white dove — to meet the royal messengers."

The mother wiped her tears with her apron, and, having understood her husband's intention, carefully took out the whitest dove out of the dovecot, and brought her to the reptiles.

The snake deputation hissed contentedly, put the dove into a little basket, and set out towards the lake.

There was a lonely birch standing behind the village with a cuckoo sitting on it. When the cuckoo spotted the delegation, she started crying out:

> *"Cuckoo, cuckoo, cuckoo,*
> *Aren't you a silly crew!*
> *They gave you no fine love,*
> *But a little white dove,*
> *Cuckoo, cuckoo, cuckoo!"*

The reptiles stopped their progress, and sullenly returned to the homestead.

"This is not the real bride!" hissed the best man and returned the dove to the farmer.

The farmer was full of apologies. "This must have been my wife's mistake. Indeed, we have three daughters, and they are all of a lovely white colour. Don't be angry, she'll bring you the real one in no time."

He gave his wife a knowing look, the farmer's wife understood, and brought a pretty plump goose. The deputation accepted it, and once again set out on its way to the lake.

On the birch past the village the cuckoo was waiting for them, and once again she mocked them:

> *"Cuckoo, cuckoo, cuckoo,*
> *Aren't you a foolish crew!*
> *It's not a gentle bride you've got,*
> *But a goose to cook in a pot,*
> *Cuckoo, cuckoo, cuckoo!"*

The snake delegation gave an angry hiss, and once again returned to the homestead. The thick snake spoke harshly to the farmer. "Again you wanted to fool us. This time you must give us the right daughter, or there will be trouble!"

"Don't be cross, esteemed guests," the farmer tried to soothe their anger. "Did I not tell you I have three daughters? How do I know which one promised to become your king's wife? I will then bring you the third, my most beloved little sheep."

And indeed, he brought with him a lovely white sheep. At once the snakes set out for the lake, but there was the cuckoo already waiting for them on the birch. And she sang:

> *"Cuckoo, cuckoo, cuckoo,*
> *Aren't you a silly crew!*
> *They gave you a funny bride,*
> *A sheep to trot at your king's side,*
> *Cuckoo, cuckoo, cuckoo!"*

This time the snakes got really angry. They left the sheep where she was, and hastened back to the farm.

The thick-set best man hissed at the farmer with such fury that he spluttered poisonous saliva all over the place. "What a treacherous fellow you are! We came to you as an honest deputation and you keep deceiving us! If you don't give us the true bride this time, we shall make you perish! When I wave my tail to the left, the snakes will pounce upon your orchards, gnaw away all the bark from your trees, and you shall have no fruit. It is enough for me to wave my tail to the right, and all the reptiles will crawl to the lake across your fields, and you shall not harvest a single grain of corn. If I just raise my head a little, all our adders will settle in your well, and you shall not have a pint of drinking water. So what is it going to be? Will you give us the true bride this time, or not?"

The farmer was frightened, but at that very moment Egle, having well heard what the wedding guests were threatening to do, ran out, embraced her father, and said, crying, "Yesterday I gave my word to the water-snake at the lake that

I would become his wife. Well, now I must keep my promise. There is nothing else to be done." It was indeed a sad leave-taking — all cries, sighs, embracings, and then tears and nothing but tears. Afterwards the snake delegation set out to the lake taking the bride with them. Behind the village on the birch the cuckoo welcomed them again:

> *"Cuckoo, cuckoo, cuckoo,*
> *Now it's the bride good and true*
> *That you're taking to your lord.*
> *Yesterday she gave her word.*
> *Cuckoo, cuckoo, cuckoo."*

When the wedding party reached the lake, the main best man raised his head, and hissed with all his might, "King of the Lake, our lord and master! Here is your chosen bride!"

At those words, the water surface rippled and a big black snake appeared. The moment he touched the bank, he turned into a handsome young man clad in a magnificent robe with a golden crown on his head. He smiled at the maiden and said, "I am Zhaltys, King of the Lake. Yesterday I took a fancy to you, and you promised to become my wife. Do you then really wish to have me for your husband?"

Egle looked at the comely young man. She found him very handsome and likeable. She bent her head and said quietly, "Yes, I shall be happy to marry you, and will walk beside you as long as I live."

Thereupon the bridegroom took his bride to the palace made of conches at the bottom of the lake, and a gorgeous wedding was celebrated. Then the young newly-weds lived happily together, and it seemed that nothing could disturb their cheerful and calm married life. When one is happy, one feels that time flies like the wind. And that is how it seemed to Egle. Before she knew, she had spent nine years down in the Conch Palace.

By that time she had already given birth to three children, two sons who were strong and handsome like their father, and a little daughter who was lovely and gentle like her mother, always smiling happily like the sun in the sky. The queen was proud of her lovely and good children. All of a sudden, she was seized by a desire to go and tell her father and mother and sisters how happy she was. But her husband would not hear of it. And Egle knew it would be useless to try to persuade him to let her go.

One day when the ninth year was drawing to its close, a white dove circled over the lake and called to Egle in a sad voice that she should return home quickly, as her father was dying.

The queen begged her husband to let her go and see her father, but he would not allow her to do so. The next day, there was a white goose swimming on the lake, and moaning plaintively that the farmer was about to die, and that he kept asking for Egle, his dearest daughter, to come to him.

Once again the queen begged her husband to let her go and see her father.

"I must still consider it all very carefully," Zhaltys said, when he saw his wife's unhappy face.

On the third day a white sheep came to the shore of the lake, and bleated so woefully that a stone would have taken pity on her.

"You must hurry up, dear queen, if you want to find your father still alive. Cold sweat is already coming out on his forehead."

Egle started crying, and her tears softened her husband's heart. "Dear Egle," he said, "you have been a good wife to me for full nine years, so you deserve to visit your parents now. But mind you are back in nine days!"

"You will surely allow me to take the children with me. I should like to show them to everybody to make them see how happy we have been living together here," the queen declared and called the children to join her.

"When you are returning on the ninth day take care there is no one to see you off. Then you will call to me softly from the shore:

> Zhaltys, my only husband true,
> Come up from your depth of green and blue!
> The children are yearning for you,
> Your wife is pining for you.

"Children, you must never give away these words, or even my name, to anyone. If you do, we shall never meet again," the father bade them rather sadly.

"My dear wife, the moment you call me with these words on the ninth day, the lake will ripple into silvery foam, and I will come swimming to take you down. But if the surface is blood red, it will be a sign for you that a very bad misfortune has befallen me," said the king gently. Then he changed into a long black snake, the queen and the children sat on his back, and he bore them up from the depth direct to the sandy shore.

"Do not forget, my dear," said Zhaltys to his wife, when he had assumed human shape again, "that you also have the power to change. Should any evil befall you, you can turn yourself and the children into anything you like."

Then they all kissed one another goodbye and parted.

When they arrived at her father's house her brothers and sisters surrounded her and admired her lovely, gentle children and her precious royal garment. Her father got well from sheer joy. He sat down joyfully at the festive table, and there was no end of feasting, telling stories, asking questions again and again, story-telling and feasting until the break of day.

However, you know what the evil tongues of envious neighbours are capable of. At once they fell to gossiping, overflowing with venomous slander.

"Egle has made a very good match indeed, hasn't she? And how proudly she bears herself!"

"She is a queen now, but there is water dripping from her brocade garments."

"And what's more, if you have noticed, she smells of fish, poor thing, fie!"

"Her children are pretty as a picture, but they are said to have fishy scales instead of nails, and lobster's claws instead of ears, poor things!"

They made a point of talking rather loudly so that all the villagers should hear it.

Of course, these tales were certain to reach the ears of Egle's brothers, and they took them very much to heart. They felt ashamed of their relatives from the lake. They came up to their sister and tried to impress on her that she should not humiliate them, should not go back to the lake, and that she and her children ought to stay there with them.

"That's impossible, don't you see, my dear foolish brothers," laughed Egle at her brothers' suggestions. "How could I leave my beloved husband? How could I deprive the children of their kind father?"

"Well, tell us at least your royal husband's name, and we will call him up at the lake for a little chat. Then we shall be sure to persuade him to give you freedom."

"I will tell you nothing, and stop tormenting me!" said the angry Egle turning her back on her brothers. They knew it was all in vain to try and get any secret out of their sister.

Then the elder brother hit upon a terrible idea. "What about questioning the children?" he suggested. "They usually blurt out everything they hear tell at home."

"Well, it certainly is worth trying," agreed the others, and that very evening they set out to graze the horses by night. They took Egle's elder son with them. He was overjoyed to go, for he had never been to a pasture before, and he loved the prancing grey horses.

The brothers bound the horses' front legs to prevent them from running far, made a fire at the edge of the forest, sat round it baking potatoes, and asked the boy a lot of questions about the lake kingdom. The boy was willing to tell his uncles what he knew, but when they asked him about his father's name, he would not say a word. Unable to get anything out of him by fair means, they tried to make him talk by using foul ones. But however hard they lashed the boy with a rod, they never prized a single word out of him.

"He is stubborn like his mother," said one of the uncles, and after this they paid no further attention to the boy. When they got home from the pasture in the morning, Egle noticed that the boy was pale and his eyes were red.

"Did the uncles hurt you in any way, my son?" she asked anxiously.

"By no means," said the boy bravely. "I was putting logs and brushwood on the fire, and so my eyes turned a bit red with tears."

Next day the brothers again set out on a night grazing expedition. This time it was the smaller boy they took with them. They subjected him to questioning by fair means and foul, but he did not tell them his father's name. Though they broke a rod by beating him, the boy kept silent as a grave.

He, too, hid his troubles from his mother by blaming the smoke when she looked searchingly into his tear-reddened eyes.

The third evening the brothers took their little niece to the pasture to give her a chance to enjoy baking potatoes, while grazing the gentle horses. The little girl had always been her father's pet. No one had ever done her any harm, or even given her a bad look. Sitting by the fire, she prattled merrily, but when the uncles started asking her for her father's name, she got scared and resisted with tears in her eyes:

"I must never tell you that. Daddy said that a misfortune would befall us if I did."

"This is probably what he meant by that misfortune," grinned one of the uncles, and swished the little girl's legs with the rod. The little thing cried bitterly, and when he swished her a second time, she told her uncles everything they wished to know.

After this the brothers quickly put out the fire, ran the horses into a herd and returned home. Now they knew the secret of the King of the Lake. Without even going to sleep, they went out with scythes towards the lake. Once there and using the agreed-on words, they called Zhaltys out from the lake, and when the big black snake appeared in the silvery brine, they fell upon him and killed him. Then they washed their blood-stained scythes in the lake and went home.

As they were hanging up the scythes in the shed, one of the scythes dropped on the stony floor, and its steel blade gave a ring as when a bell is struck. Egle heard it, and terrified she ran out into the courtyard, and saw her brothers putting away the scythes.

"I got scared that it was a death-knell tolling for somebody, and it is just you clanking your scythes. Don't tell me you were out mowing!" she said in astonishment, but her heart was assailed by a strange feeling of anxiety. She was unable to drive off the woeful tinkling of the passing bell.

"We have done all the mowing now," said the eldest brother casually. "You know very well there is a lot of dew at daybreak, and it is the best time to mow."

Why, of course, that is what Egle knew only too well, but do what she might she was unable to overcome the feeling of unrest and anxiety.

No sooner were the children awake than she bade farewell to her parents and her brothers and sisters, and did not allow anyone to see them off. She took the children, and hastily, as if pursued by some evil spirits, ran to the lake with them. Once on the shore, and all out of breath, she called those words:

> *"Zhaltys, my only husband true,*
> *Come up from your depth of green and blue.*
> *The children are yearning for you,*
> *Your wife is pining for you."*

For a moment all was silent — like a calm before a storm. Then all of a sudden the water in the lake surged up and the red-coloured waves brought blood-stained foam to the shore.

The queen wept bitterly. She knew that a terrible misfortune had happened. And suddenly a very sorrowful voice came up from the depths of the lake:

> *"I met my death at the hands of evil men,*
> *Because of your fright, my daughter dear,*

Since the lash filled you with fear.
Your brothers stood firm like rocks
Resisting all the wiles and guiles,
Never giving away a single word
To the uncles, those foul murderers.
Goodbye to you, my dear ones, farewell!"

It was only then that poor Egle realized what great misfortune had befallen them. She stopped crying, and said to her children: "We have been afflicted by a great sorrow. You have lost your father and I my beloved husband. Now we can never return to the realm of the lake, nor can we even think of going back to your grandfather's farm. For could we possibly live under one roof with murderers? We will stay here on the shore so that we can always look into those depths where we used to be so happy together.

"You, my eldest son, will now turn into a spreading hard oak, because you firmly resisted the murderers and did not give away anything. You, my younger son, will be a resilient ash tree, because you, too, knew how to resist. As for you, my dearest little daughter, I will change you into a timid aspen tree, and you shall always shake and tremble as you trembled with fear before you gave away your father's name. Myself I will turn into a weeping willow, bend my head over the surface of the lake, and mourn the death of my darling husband."

And as she said, so it was done. To this day there are four magnificent large trees standing on the shore of that lake. The oak and the ash tree have mighty strong stems. They proudly withstand all the onslaughts of strong winds, and protect the other two trees by their spreading crowns: the timid, ever-trembling aspen, and the weeping willow which bends woefully over the lake. On silent starry nights her long soft branches gently stroke the rippling water surface.

The Cock and the Hen

A cock and a hen lived together in a farmyard. Truth to tell, the hen was rather a silly, cackling and mean hen, and she would go and spy on the cock, and do her worst to annoy him.

One day the cock suddenly felt like eating some nuts. So he set out for the backyard where the hazel stood, and the hen at once went after him, of course. After awhile, they came to the hazel tree, but the nuts grew too high and the hen could not reach them.

"You must pluck them for me yourself!" she yelled at the poor cock. "But mind you get me only the biggest and the sweetest ones. Otherwise, I am going to complain to the farmer."

The good-hearted cock only nodded, and set to picking nuts for all he was worth. The hen immediately gobbled them up without considering that the cock had not yet tasted a single one. In the end, there was only one nut left on the hazel, but it was so high that not even the cock was able to reach it.

"Go on, go on," cackled the hen, but this at last made the cock mightily cross.

"Don't you see how high it is?" he said angrily.

"Well, jump up, or I will tell on you that you wanted to cheat me!"

"Oh, what a nuisance," thought the cock to himself, but jumped up to reach the nut, notwithstanding.

Goodness knows how it happened, but instead of falling down on the ground, the nut hit the hen straight on the head. Oh, what lamentations followed this mishap!

"You wanted to kill me! You've put my eye out!" yelled the hen staggering straight into the farmyard.

The farmer was just standing in the porch, so the hen at once acted as if she was on the point of dying.

Of course, the cock did not feel much like going home, for the moment he stepped into the yard, the farmer seized a big stick and shouted roughly at him:

"Well, how was it with those nuts?"

"The hazel tree dropped the last one on the hen's head," answered the cock.

So the farmer bade the hazel to appear before him — why had she done such a terrible thing?

"I had not the slightest intention, farmer, but how am I to manage to drop a nut where I want to when I am all shaking with cold after the goat has gnawed away all my bark?"

"So it's the goat's fault, is it?" said the farmer to himself.

However, the goat, too, had an excuse:

"How am I not to gnaw away the bark when the goatherd did not take me out to the meadow?"

So the goatherd had to come out with the truth, but it was a truth that cut to the quick. What he said was:

"I should have been glad to take the goat to pasture, but the housekeeper had promised me biscuits and gave me nothing. How can I be expected to graze cattle on an empty stomach?"

Now the farmer was near to giving up in despair. So it was his own wife who was to blame for all this.

"Why didn't you give the goatherd the biscuits you had promised to give him?" he shouted into the kitchen through the open window.

"You are one to ask," was the reply from inside. "Was it not you who ate them all up yourself to the last morsel?"

The farmer stood thunderstruck, his eyes flaming, and his head all in turmoil.

"So that in the end it's me ..." he started after a while to feel embarrassed, but suddenly his eyes came to rest on the hen who, without a trace of any wound, was happily rooting in the ground for grains. This was the last straw.

"You shall be sorry for your eternal complaints!" he exclaimed, swooped upon the hen, and wrung her neck. Then he handed her to his wife, and ordered: "Put that damned beast in the frying pan. She was only mislaying eggs anyway, always raising complaints against everybody, and now she wants to get even me into trouble!"

So that was the end of the good-for-nothing hen, and serves her right, too. No one was sorry for her except the cock, whom she had wronged most while she lived. But that is the way things sometimes happen.

The Tale of the Mirror

Once upon a time in ancient fairy-tale days, human habitations were miles and miles away from each other. And since they were separated by wide rivers and impenetrable forests with no paths even for the deer, people stayed in their cottages all alone and many of them hardly ever set eyes on an unknown face in their lives unless a wanderer happened to come their way.

Of course, they were not all alike, and even in such remote God-forsaken corners of the earth many knew well that beyond the forests and rivers not only whole villages, but even towns with stone walls and houses and churches were to be found.

One of these was Lavri, who was living in a remote little cottage with his parents and his pretty young wife. Once in the winter season when he went to the forest to fetch wood, he met an unknown hunter, who told him about the great city. He talked about the lords and ladies who rode in carriages, and how everyone dressed up in outlandish clothes — not like Lavri in his unwieldy sheepskin; about people who made merry over good food, drinking or listening to music — entirely incredible things.

The poor cottager was exceedingly inquisitive, so after meeting the man he went about pondering what the hunter had told him. In the end, his curiosity get the better of him and he decided to go and see these things with his own eyes, no matter how long the journey to the city should take.

However, his people would not let him go; his wife groaned, his mother kept lamenting, and the old father mumbled something about high-fallutin' ideas adding that he was none the less happy for never having seen a city in his life.

In the end, however, Lavri had his way. In the spring, no sooner had the snow melted a little and the wolves retired deeper into the forest, than he saddled the only poor little horse they had, and set out to see the world.

A long, long time had he ridden before he reached a road, and even longer before he set his eyes on stone walls. He passed through the gate all set to contemplate the marvellous buildings and palaces, to watch the noble burghers and lovely ladies, admire the bustle in the streets, the splendid garments and the choice food that people were feasting on in ordinary inns and which he had never even tasted.

However, he was soon to discover that, while at home in the cottage they never even knew what money was, because nobody ever needed it, here in the city you could not do without it.

Lavri did not have to rack his brains long before he figured out how to earn money.

"I can drive a horse, whether put to the waggon or under the saddle," he said to himself, and so he offered himself as a cartman to the first man he met.

His luck was in — the man was a rich merchant who was just looking for a good cartman. They exchanged a few words, and since the merchant was no miser and what he mainly required of the peasant was honesty, they soon struck a bargain.

For a whole year Lavri transported all kinds of goods for the merchant, and worked so hard that his master had nothing but praise for him. So when the cartman began feeling homesick, the master did all he could to persuade him to stay on.

But Lavri was restless. So in return for his services the merchant gave him a light coach full of clothes, boots, precious spices and many other things besides, adding a little sack full of golden coins. As he was bidding the peasant farewell he put a little mirror in his pocket.

"What are you giving me this for?" asked Lavri in surprise. "You have bestowed enough gifts on me as it is. And where I come from nobody knows anyway what mirrors are good for."

At this the merchant only laughed. "That is exactly why. When everyone in the cottage has come to terms with the mirror you may come back to me after all, and bring your family as well. In a year's time I shall be expecting you."

Lavri was perplexed with these words, and all the way home he thought about them. But what they were supposed to mean he could not divine.

Do you think his people at home were pleased with his gifts? Well, his wife was happy to see him back at last, and pleased with the lovely jewels as well, but his father and mother only upbraided him for having been away so long on his travels, when he knew how badly he was needed at home. As to the gifts he had brought, they did not even glance at them.

Lavri was disappointed, but worse was to come. When his wife was putting away his new coat the next day, the mirror fell out of the pocket, and she at once had a look at it.

"Alas, alas," she started lamenting. "Now that's why Lavri was so long in coming back. And he thinks nothing of bringing her picture with him, the cheeky beggar!"

The mother heard the wife's complaint, and of course she wondered what was afoot.

"Lavri has got some fair young woman in the town — he even brought her picture with him, just have a look," sighed the wife, handing the mirror to his mother.

But when the mother looked into the mirror, she fell to lamenting even more: "What are you talking about? She is a perfect old hag, so many wrinkles she has got! Oh, Lavri, Lavri, how could you have been so blind!"

Now they were crying together.

The father, hearing their cries, rushed into the room all out of breath, and the old mother at once blurted out, "Come and look what shame Lavri has heaped upon us. He has found himself such a hag for a sweetheart in the town, and what's more, he kept her picture!"

The old man took the mirror, looked, and very nearly had a stroke. "What kind of a hag? Why, that is some ugly old man I can see there . . . My son must have gone mad in the town!"

Thus they went on crying, moaning and lamenting, all three of them, till they made the dog in the courtyard howl. And that was how Lavri found them on coming back from the field in the evening.

At once his wife, mother and father swooped upon him all pointing at the mirror at the same time. And indeed, it took him rather a long time to get to the bottom of the thing. However, having done so, he burst out laughing. "It was your own faces you were looking at! That is no picture, but quite a simple little mirror, a thing that every fool in the city knows!" And at once Lavri put his own face in front of the wondrous thing, and each of the three had to look over his shoulder to see Lavri in the mirror.

When they came to understand what that picture was good for, they all looked ashamed and then they began to question Lavri about the way people lived in the city, and what he had done, seen and experienced there.

There was so much to tell and to listen to that it took a whole week. And at the end of the week no one was willing to stay another day in the cottage. So strong was their desire to go to the city.

So Lavri struck the iron while it was hot. He put only the most necessary things on to the waggon, made his father and mother sit on the fur, his wife next to him on the box, and when he cracked his whip to make his horse set out to the merchant and a better living, he understood very well why he had been given that ordinary mirror.

The Three Knots

That autumn dire poverty and misery descended upon the fishing village. It was as if all the fish had left the sea, and day after day the fishermen came home without any catch in their nets. And an empty fishing net, that is like an empty barn — both of them yawn with hunger.

When distress and want had started to settle down in all the huts, the fishermen decided to go and see old Kaarel begging him to advise them where to go fishing. Kaarel was not an ordinary old man; he was an experienced mariner, a whale harpooner in his young days who had sailed probably all the oceans of the world. He lived like a recluse behind the village. Every one respected him for his wisdom, and many came to seek his advice.

"There are times when fish avoid nets," said Kaarel, having heard his neighbours' complaints. Then he knocked the ashes out of his short pipe and went on, "Before spring returns, fish will again be passing through our waters, and until then you just have to tighten your belts. You simply have to survive."

"We have been tightening our belts for a long time now," a red-haired fisherman blurted out. "But what about our children? They are on the point of starving and wasting away before our eyes. We really can't wait till spring comes."

"That is true," agreed Kaarel. "The children must not be allowed to starve."

He mused a while and then said, "I will help you, and if you do exactly as I say, you will find at least some relief."

"We knew, Kaarel, that you would not leave us in the lurch. And we will do everything you say," shouted the fishermen.

At this, Kaarel opened a chest, and after rummaging inside for a while, finally pulled out a faded red silk scarf. He stroked it gently, and handed it to the fishermen with a smile. "This is a scarf I have worn round my neck all my life, and I have never been let down by fishermen's luck. I got it one day from the Queen of the Seas herself. I will let you have the magic scarf, but be careful!

"As you can see, there are three knots on it. When you untie the first knot, a favourable wind will rise and fill your sails. If you untie the second knot, all the nets will fill with fish up to the brim. But you must make do with the first pull and must not throw the net into the sea again. And as to the third knot — that one you must never untie. It would bring you bad luck if you did."

The fishermen took the faded red scarf from the old harpooner and said, "Don't be afraid, we shall never untie the third knot, here is our mariner's word upon it."

"All right, all right, a mariner is always as good as his word," said the old man with a smile, lighting his pipe. "You would only be harming yourselves and your children should you not listen to me."

And so they parted in good accord. The very next day the fishermen set out on a fishing expedition. They loaded the nets on to the largest boat, and having set sails made for the open sea. No sooner had they left the haven than the helmsman untied the first knot on the scarf. And right enough, a sharp wind rose, the sails swelled, and the boat shot forward like an arrow. The way its mighty prow cut the wave tops was a pleasure to see. The mariners burst into song; they hoped their fishing trip would be a success this time. They had been sailing a whole half a day under the swelling sails. They had lost sight of the shore, and found themselves far out on the open sea. After a time the wind dropped, the sails went limp, and the ship came to a standstill.

"Here we shall probably strike on the fish," cried the helmsman, "be quick, lads, and drop the anchor!"

So they lowered the anchor and spread the nets. The helmsman untied the second knot and at that moment the water surface round the ship started rippling and phosphorescing as thousands upon thousands of silvery-backed fishes crowded the nets. The fishermen gazed in amazement at the miracle, and were at a loss as to what to do first.

"Well, lads, get hold of the nets and haul in very, very slowly. Not a single little fish must be wasted," cried the wise helmsman.

The fishermen recovered from their surprise and slowly and very gently hauled the nets on board. Heavens, what a haul that was, what a yield! Before long the hold was full of living, scaly silver.

"Another haul and we'll have more than ever before," exclaimed a young fisherman eagerly.

"But Kaarel told us to cast the nets only once, and we gave him our word," warned the helmsman.

The red-haired fisherman gave an evil laugh:

"Old Kaarel is far away, and there are such a lot of fish all around that it would be a sin to leave them in the sea!"

The others joined in, shouted down the helmsman, and cast the nets into the sea again. But wonder of wonders! This time not a single little fish got caught in the net.

Though disappointed the fishermen would not give up. As if possessed they kept casting the nets into the sea, but every time they hauled them out empty! Only some seaweed and a few mussels got caught in the nets.

"This can't be true," said the mariners in astonishment. "There must be some charm behind this!"

The red-headed man turned sharply to the helmsman:

"Be quick, untie the third knot!"

"That I will never do," the helmsman defied him. "For we gave Kaarel our mariner's word that we would not, don't you remember?"

The sailors were taken aback, but the man would not give in.

"Well, come on. Two knots have helped us, so shall the third. Hurry up and untie that third knot!" insisted even the other fishermen.

The helmsman would not stand for it, but in the end they pulled the scarf out of his hand, and the red-headed man boldly untied the last knot.

At that moment a terrible storm broke out over the sea and they only just managed to roll up the sails. Waves as big as castles were mounting, beating against the gunwales and flooding the board. Suddenly, all the fishermen were busy rushing about helter-skelter, not knowing what to do: weigh the anchor, fold the sails, or bail the water out of the hold. The first thing to do was to haul in the nets so that the surf should not carry them away. But it was too late. Try as they might, they just could not haul the nets out of the water. The nets had got stuck in the depths as if held fast by something enormous. And so they were!

All at once the nets went taut, and the fishermen were horrified to see a giant fish entangled in them, possibly a whale. As if out of her senses, she was trying to escape from her bondage, and the harder she tried, the more entangled she became. Finally she thrust herself forward together with the net, and tearing out the anchor, pulled the fishing boat behind her like a feather.

The gale was howling in the ropes, the masts groaning and breaking. The fishermen were either cursing the sea, or praying to St. Peter, their patron saint. The helmsman tied himself to the helm lest a wave should wash him overboard, and tried in vain to steer the boat, which, hauled by the whale, was riding like mad over the mountains of the waves into the dark unknown where the stormy sea blended with the black clouds. Fiery lines of lightning crossed the skies.

In one of the flashes the fishermen saw a rugged rock in the distance in front of them. And towards it the whale was heading with the boat in tow. Now we are lost! thought the fishermen, crossing themselves. At the last moment, the helmsman, putting all his strength into the effort, seized the helm — and the boat missed the rock by a hair's breadth. Suddenly the boat calmed down, and slowly came to a halt. The whale must have fought free of the net and escaped.

The fishermen heaved a sigh of relief. Not far behind the rock they noticed a bit of dry land, perhaps a little island. A moment later, the boat's keel grated on the sandy bottom, and the boat got stuck near the shore.

The fishermen got out, and looked round the deserted island. They had never been there before, and there did not seem to be a living soul anywhere. Then they noticed a faint, yellowish light. They set out towards it in the rain, and at last they reached a small fisherman's hovel.

Before they recovered from their surprise, the door opened, and there was a tiny old man standing on the threshold. The long years had made him bend forward a great deal, so that his white beard fell down to his knees. But the old man's eyes were full of fire like those of a young man and of kindness, like those of every good man.

"Well, come in, lads, don't stand out there in the rain," he said welcoming them, and opening the door wide. "I knew you were coming all wet and frozen, so I made a fire in the room and some tea for you."

The stiff fishermen did not wait to be urged. In a moment they filled the cosy warm room to the last corner.

After the first glass of hot tea they recovered a little, and started questioning their good-hearted host:

What kind of an island was it, for they had never heard of it, and how was it possible that the old man had been expecting them?

The old man smoothed his silvery beard contentedly and said:

"There is rarely a gale in these parts. The Queen of the Seas must get awfully angry to make the waves rise so high and the wild wind roar as it does today. And when hell gets loose like this, when the sea gets torn away from its chains, then usually a ship lands on my island. Believe it or not, this is a magic island. Sailors always discover it at the right time to save their skins. That is why I was expecting you to come for sure today. And what was it you fellows did to offend our Queen of the Seas? Just come clean and tell me all about it."

The fishermen, sipping the hot tea, felt ashamed and kept silent. Then the helmsman plucked up courage, and recounted to the old man how they had been afflicted with great misery and hunger, and old Kaarel helped them with his good advice and his magic scarf.

"I know old Kaarel very well," said the old man. "We fished together for years. I remember he was wearing a silk scarf round his neck. It was a gift from the Queen of the Seas herself. Show me that scarf, my friend."

The helmsman produced the precious scarf from his pocket, and handed it to the old man.

"Yes, that's the one," said the old man beaming with pleasure. "Only there were always three knots on it if I am not mistaken."

The helmsman sadly nodded:

"You are right, grandpa, there were three knots on it. The first when untied put the wind into our sails. The second drove lots of fish into our nets. And the third — Kaarel had warned us, we must never untie that onc. We gave him our mariner's word, but we did not keep it."

"Well, well," said the old man gloomily, "that is what happens when a mariner breaks his word. You have brought upon your heads the just ire of the Queen of the Seas. Therefore she sent down that gale on you, therefore she let loose the whale to upset your boat. Good job that the monster got entangled in your nets."

The fishermen felt terrible in the presence of the old man, and a sincere regret for not having kept their mariner's word.

"What should we do now?" they lamented. "The gale is still raging outside, and at home our wives are crying with fear and our children with hunger."

"You must stay the night here, and in the morning we shall see," said the old man to comfort them. So they slept anywhere they could: on the table, on the benches, even on the floor. But in the morning there were still streams of rain pouring down from the sky, and the raging sea was frightening.

The old man was the first to rise. He made the fire, prepared breakfast and combed his silvery beard. When he saw how unhappy and miserable his lodgers looked, he took pity on them, and said, "You have had your measure of suffering, but it serves you right, I don't feel sorry for you at all. But for the sake of your poor children, and because I am fond of my friend Kaarel, I am now going to help you. Let me have the scarf!"

They gave him the scarf, and he went out into the doorway, waved it towards the sea, and once again tied the third knot they had been forbidden ever to untie.

That very moment the gale subsided, the rain stopped, and the sun's rays pierced the clouds like golden arrows. The fishermen ran to their boat, put right the rigging, hauled out the torn nets, hoisted the sails, and made ready to set out.

The old man went to see them off, and the grateful mariners bade him farewell. The moment he waved them goodbye from the shore, a wind rose from his palms, filling the sails, and the fishing boat flew like a seagull over the surface, straight home. Before evening fell they had reached their native harbour.

The whole village was rejoicing when the fishermen returned safely, bringing a rich catch with them. So many fish would be enough to feed them until spring came again. There would be no scourge of hunger and want.

After this, all the children in the village learnt to tie firm knots, and would tie them wherever they could: on a piece of string, on a rope, on a handkerchief, even on stockings. And they would say as they did it, "This knot will never give way. It is as firm as a mariner's word."

The Horse and the Gnat

On a luscious meadow in the bend of a quiet stream a little horse was grazing —
a gentle young bay horse with wise eyes. All of a sudden there came a gnat
buzzing above his head. He settled between the horse's ears, and gave a quarrelsome squeak. "You're overfeeding, unwieldy creature! Look what a sizeable belly
you've grown from eating so much grass!"

The horse only tossed his head, shook off the importunate gnat, and went on
grazing contentedly. But the gnat would not leave him in peace. He settled on
a nearby bush and came out with threats. "You shall suffer for having thrown me,
you lout! I'll show you!"

But the horse took no notice. He went on quietly eating the green grass and
paid no àttention to the gnat. The latter was furious like the devil, and went on
angrily:

"So you won't even deign to answer me, you fat belly! Just you wait, I'll teach
you good manners!"

He sat down on the horse's rump and tried to pierce the horse's hide with his
sharp proboscis. But his efforts were in vain.

The bay horse did not like being tickled, so he just waved his tail, and swept the gnat off into the grass. This was too much for the gnat to put up with. So he smoothed out his crumpled little wings, and yelled, as he flew round the horse's head, "So this is what you do, you swollen-headed ruffian! You are not afraid of me, because I am of a small stature, but man is also smaller than you are, and when he cracks the whip, you're scared. Well, that man is terribly scared of me. The moment I give a squeak, he waves his arms about and tries to run away from me, you see. He knows what an implacable fighter I am."

The horse lifted his head, looked askance at the importunate little fellow, and calmly went on grazing. The gnat was beside himself with anger, and whistled straight into the horse's ear till he nearly lost his voice, "So, you continue to ignore me? We gnats are a mere nothing for you, are we? You go on offending us like this? On behalf of all gnats I declare war on you!"

"Now you are bragging," snorted the horse without giving him a single look.

"I will call our glorious army, and we shall sting you to death!" the gnat yelled.

"Get you gone, you piping whipper-snapper, before I really lose my temper," neighed the horse, and bent his head down to the green turf again.

"Oh, what an abominable cheek! Just wait, you fat villain, this will cost you dear! Such a shame can only be washed off with blood!" whistled the gnat, and flew straight off to fetch the whole army of gnats.

A moment later, the sky above the bay horse grew dark, there was a rustle like a waterfall, and a mighty swarm of gnats prepared themselves for an attack.

"Into battle, into battle, comrades! Beat the enemy, show no mercy! He dares to ignore us. He dares to offend us! So let him perish!" yelled the gnat in his high-pitched voice, having proclaimed himself leader of the host.

"Death to the enemy! Hurrah!" shouted the enraged gnats, gallantly pushing out their proboscises, and they alighted on the horse like a thundering cloud.

For a while, he drove the gnats off with his tail, then he shook his mane impatiently several times, but they kept on attacking, in wave after wave, and had already occupied the whole of his back. This made the horse lose his temper a little. So he lay down in the grass and rolled over from side to side several times until all the gnats were crushed.

One gnat survived the battle. He straightened his ruffled wings, and using his last bit of strength, flew up to the leader, who was watching the progress of the battle from a distant bush, and reported to him, "Our leader, we have won! We have struck the horse down, he is lying with his legs in the air, and wallowing in a deadly spasm."

The leader thanked the brave gnat for his joyful news, promised to award him a high military order, and hastened to leave the battlefield.

He flew up to the nearest tree, where he had hidden his silver trumpet, and seizing it, blazoned abroad into the wide world:

"A triumph! A triumph! We have won the war! The enemy is totally defeated! Eternal glory to us, the gnats, the bravest soldiers in the world!"

Meanwhile the horse, the wise, gentle bay, went on grazing contentedly on the luscious meadow in the bend of the quiet stream.

Why Owls Hoot

When you stroll through the forest today you may assume that the solemn still-ness and peace has been there from time immemorial. Quite the reverse is true.

The story goes that far back in primeval times the woods resounded with noise and din. The animals made hardly any noise — but the birds! They have always been a restless and quarrelsome lot.

In those days every bird sang as he liked. Whatever sound he heard, he at once tried to imitate it, and the others aped him, each trying to outdo the others. This caused no end of confusion. All the voices got mixed up, as if knotted together. All at once the nightingale croaked, the magpie twittered, the eagle cuckooed, the crow chirped — well, it was a pretty kettle of fish, as the saying goes.

Woe to the person who had to cross the forest in those times. If he did not pull his cap down over his ears in time, he was sure to go deaf from the birds' hullabaloo.

Well, one day the noise set the bear thinking. Acting as mayor in the forest at the time, he liked his little snooze when work was over and the birds' uproar often disturbed his sleep. So he determined to put some order into the birds' singing. Well, you know the bear. What he takes into his round head to have done, that is sure to be done.

So one day he called all the birds together to a large clearing, seated himself on an oak barrel which he had rolled to that spot from his lair, waved his paw to gain silence, and said, "I will be brief — there must be peace, quiet and order in the forest. You simply cannot whistle, croak and twitter all the time, any old way you like. Look, I have rolled in a barrel full of birds' songs. You choose a tune after your taste and bill. But remember: Once you have chosen your song, you shall always sing that, and no other! As from today I do not wish to hear, say, the magpie trying to crow. You understand?"

The birds understood their hairy mayor very well. He had clearly explained what things were going to be like from then on, and they knew he was not to be trifled with.

They came flying to the enormous oak barrel, the bear pulled out the thick plug from the bottom, and at once there were birds' songs popping out of the opening one after the other. The birds picked one each to suit their bills, the colour of their feathers, and to please their fancy. There was some gobbling and chattering but only very, very little; no one wanted to incur the lord mayor's displeasure.

By midday, every bird had his own song; only the owls had not put in an appearance. This, of course, caused no surprise, for owls are known to sleep through the day, sluggards as they are, and only towards evening do they become sociable.

And that was exactly what happened this time. In the evening, having learnt that every bird had got his own tune, they hastened to the clearing to obtain a song as well. Of course, they came when the show was over. All they found was the empty barrel. The tunes had been divided among the other birds, and there was nothing at all left for the sleepy owls.

They felt sad and did not know what to do. The oldest and wisest owl gave this advice: "There is nothing left for us now but to fly off to men. They are always singing, they have no end of songs. Perhaps they will let us have one or two."

The other owls agreed, and at once flew to the village. It was well after midnight and there was light only in a single cottage. There happened to be a wedding celebration there. In the small hours most of the guests were overcome by sleep. Some slept on the table and under the table, women were dozing on the oven, the musicians on the benches. Only in the corner the last of the fiddlers held his double-bass, sleepily passing the bow over the single string still left after the music-making. There was nothing but ever the same deep tone coming out of the double-bass, just a long, sad hoo-hoo-hoo.

"That is the only tune left for us," said the wise owl. "It is no beauty, but it will be easy to learn."

The owls, having no choice, agreed. And their song, the sad "hoo-hoo-hoo," has been coming out of the woods ever since.

Who Calls for the Rain?

Once upon a time, a great many years ago, our Earth was afflicted with extraordinarily dry weather. From dawn to dusk the sun was scorching pitilessly. The sky was getting hotter and hotter from day to day, and not a single cloud was to be seen. The fields and meadows looked as though they were ravaged by fire, fountains and brooks dried up, all moisture sank deep into the cracked ground. Men, birds and beasts — all suffered from great thirst.

In those days a large and prudent bear was president of the forest. He was sweating profusely in the heat wave, and was always complaining about his shaggy fur coat.

One day he called all the animals and birds to gather on the foxglove clearing. When it was full, he waved his paw to make everybody quiet, and then addressed them in his booming voice:

"I am very old, but I don't remember ever having had to endure such heat and drought. We must save some water in good time, otherwise we shall all die of thirst. Now listen carefully, all of you. I'll tell you what to do. In the ravine over there we shall dig a deep pit. We may strike against a fountain but the main thing will be to wait patiently for a proper downpour. And that is sure to come before long. I can sniff it in the air even now. Then the pit will fill with rainwater, and we shall have a good supply against the time when such heat waves befall us again."

The animals and birds welcomed their president's wise words, and set to work without delay to dig a pit, and everybody worked as best he could.

The mole was boring ever deeper down, and reporting back to the bear: "Have struck against moist earth, am making my way through some mud, and am sure to run up against a fountain."

The fox and the wolf were using their forelegs trying side by side in good accord to burrow into the earth which the raven and the crow had dug up with their powerful beaks.

The blue-hawk and the sparrow-hawk picked stones from the pit and brought them in their claws to the dike which the stag, the roebuck and the roe together with their fawns were treading with their hoofs. The bear supervised the operations, and used his powerful paws to stamp down the bottom of the future lake. All animals and birds living in the forest worked hard, and rejoiced in their joint undertaking.

Only the oriole did nothing to help. She flew about those who were working, eyeing them curiously, and even mocking them in the end:

> *"Ticky ticky tain*
> *I'll wait for the rain;*
> *Work would make me sad,*
> *Let fools toil like mad.*
> *Won't drink water from a pit,*
> *Boring through clay will make you fit.*
> *Ticky ticky tain*
> *I'll wait for the rain."*

The birds and animals took no notice of the mocking oriole, but they thought to themselves: Just wait, we'll see who'll be the one who laughs last!

And right enough, the oriole came to a bad end.

The waterwork on which the wood-dwellers laboured proved a real success. No sooner had they finished than the sky became overcast with black clouds, and there was a huge downpour. Before long the new lake in the ravine was filled with rainwater up to the brim. Later on, when the heat and drought struck again, the animals and birds always had enough water. None of them suffered from thirst.

Only the oriole was always thirsty in that sultry season. She kept circling over the lake, she even descended towards it several times wanting to have a drink of water, but the animals and birds drove her away with their cries:

"You did not work with us, you shall not drink with us!" they said, and they were right.

Ever since then the oriole is said to be always thirsty, and only when it rains, she may allay her thirst a little. Then she is seen flying hither and thither with her

65

bill open trying to catch the raindrops, but these are hardly enough to quench her thirst! That is why the forest often resounds with her urgent little song:

"Ticky ticky tain,
Waiting for the rain."

When they hear this woeful bird's song people will say: "It is going to rain. The oriole is calling for the rain."

Good Advice beyond Price

There was once a young couple living in a village deep in the woods. The wife was busy as a bee, the husband was a good man, but none too keen on work. It was only when he really had to that he put his shoulder to the wheel. But even then he did not like work.

"Work is not a hare, it will not escape me," that was his motto, and whenever he could he lay down behind the oven.

"What a lie-abed I have got," the wife would often sigh, and did herself whatever needed doing about the house. Lie-abed became his name.

One day she crocheted a lovely wrap and said to her husband:

"Come away from the oven, you Lie-abed! Take this wrap to the market. You can ask at least three ducats for it."

"All right," yawned her husband, "I will go to town tomorrow."

"Why wait till tomorrow? You shall go at once!" said the wife angrily. "You never do a spot of work at home anyway, and only get in my way."

So Lie-abed threw the wrap over his shoulder, took his staff, and set out for the market in a sullen mood.

His journey took him through the forest. When he was approaching a crossroads, a wood-nymph suddenly appeared before him. Her little shoes were made of birch-bark, her bodice of velvet moss, her frock of lichens, and on her head was a little hat decked with cones.

Lie-abed was rather startled by the meeting, but the nymph said in a sweet soothing voice, "Have no fear. I know very well what you are taking to the market. Show me that wrap."

The man spread the wrap for the wood-nymph to look at, and she was amazed:

"Oh how lovely! What golden hands your wife has. How much do you want for it?"

"Three ducats," said the man tentatively, saying to himself he would part with it even at a cheaper price, at least it would save him a long trip to the town.

"It is not much you are asking for such a lovely thing," said the wood-nymph truthfully, "but I am afraid I have no ducats at all. However, I will pay you with good advice, which, when remembered, will bring you a lot of money one day."

Lie-abed hesitated a moment, but then said to himself that good advice is beyond price, and gave the nymph the wrap for nothing.

The wood-nymph took the wrap with a smile and then whispered to him, "When you are helping someone, you jump even into the sea, and you shall not drown."

The man liked the strange words, and took great pains to remember them.

However, even before he managed to ask the nymph what use her advice would be to him, she vanished along with the wrap as if she had melted into the air.

Lie-abed returned home merrily, but what welcome he received from his wife you can well imagine. She reproached him with everything he had ever done amiss, and belaboured him with hard words till his ears were buzzing. So he thought he'd better crawl behind the oven, and there he weathered the storm safe and sound.

In a few days the wife's just anger faded away, and having rummaged in the drawers for remnants of the knitted yarn, she crocheted a new wrap, even more beautiful than the first.

Then she roused her husband, and gave him strict orders: "Today you shall put right what you did amiss last time. Go to the market, and sell this wrap for five ducats. It is lovelier than the first. And mind you don't give it away again to a wood-nymph for a song."

So the man had to set out for the town again.

At the crossroads of the forest paths he saw the wood-nymph waiting for him already. She gave Lie-abed a friendly smile, and said impatiently:

"Show me what your skilful wife has created this time."

The man tried many dodges and excuses like a little schoolboy, but in the end the nymph did cheat him out of the magnificent wrap, and this time, too, just for a piece of good advice:

"Try to remember well," she whispered, "to look for water where the willow-tree and the grass grow!"

This time the man was none too happy about the deal, but the wood-nymph consoled him. "Have no fear, this advice will bring in much more than the five ducats you asked for the fine wrap."

Lie-abed believed her, and stored her words in his memory, but he did not feel much like going home. He loitered and loitered, and only towards evening hesitantly crossed the threshold of his house. The moment his wife looked at him, she knew that the worst had happened. If she could, she would have liked to beat him about the head with that good advice he had received in return for the lovely wrap, and he did catch a few boxes on the ears till his cap nearly jumped off.

For quite a few days the housewife did not speak a word to her husband. However, her deft hands would not leave her in peace for long. She borrowed some new yarn from her neighbour, and once again set about crocheting. The new wrap was perhaps the loveliest of the three, and it was large enough to cover two beds. She folded it in three pieces, handed it to the man, and sadly addressed him. "We have not a single groat in the house left. For this big wrap you can get as many as ten ducats. And mind you don't . . ."

"Have no fear," her husband assured her. "This time I will make sure to bring the money."

Yet not even this time did he bring it.

As could be expected, there was the wood-nymph waiting for him at the crossroads. But Lie-abed would not even talk to her. However, she was very persistent in pestering him. "At least let me see what enchanting thing your dear wife has created this time!" While trying to persuade him, she held on to his coat, and smiled so pleasantly that he eventually spread out the wrap before her.

The wood-nymph was beside herself with enthusiasm: "I must have this magnificent thing!" she cried.

This time, however, Lie-abed was as hard as the rock, and would not yield, saying that he simply could not return home without the money.

The wood-nymph begged him on bended knees, then threatened him, and ended by bursting into woeful tears. Those tears touched the man's heart, and so in the end he gave her the wrap again just for a piece of good advice, and this one was the queerest of all: "If you lift your hand in anger, never let it fall," the nymph told him, got hold of the wrap, and giving a joyful laugh, vanished as if she had dissolved into a haze.

Now, what was the poor man to do? He dared not go home empty-handed, so he set out into the wide world looking for work. He walked a long time until he reached the sea, and there he hired himself out as a cabin-boy.

He had no easy life on the ship, having to work extremely hard among the sailors. But he got accustomed to work, and in a few years he could hardly believe that at one time he had been capable of idling away whole days at home on the oven.

One day their ship got stuck on a rock. The sailors lowered a life-boat saying they would seek help on the land. They rowed and rowed until even the distant shore came into sight, but all of a sudden an enormous wave came rushing, fell over the boat and filled it with water up to the edge. They started bailing the water out but in vain, the boat was on the point of sinking.

"Somebody must be thrown overboard," yelled the helmsman. "Otherwise we shall all perish."

"Whoever volunteers to jump out of the boat, will get half of the ship's cargo," vowed the captain.

Lie-abed remembered the first piece of advice he had received from the wood-nymph, crossed himself, and jumped into the sea.

The boat got lighter and sailed safely into the harbour and all the sailors were saved.

At dawn Lie-abed came swimming to the shore as well. The sailors welcomed him as a hero, being happy he had not drowned. The captain, too, kept his promise. He gave him an honest half of the ship's cargo which was hauled into the port safely when the storm had died down.

Lie-abed sold the goods, and at once became a rich man. So he thought of his wife, how hard she must find it to scrape a few coins to keep the house going. Suddenly he felt homesick and set out for home. However, it was a long, long journey to his village. There were nine mountain ranges and seven rivers to cross. When he had crossed the last mountain range, he found himself in a kingdom which was steeped in deep mourning. All the brooks, wells and fountains there had gone dry.

The king promised a great reward to anyone who would find water. Lie-abed recalled the second piece of advice he had received from the wood-nymph, and told the king he was going to try.

So he set out on a journey round the countryside. Everything had gone dry, everywhere there was nothing but stone and cracked earth. All of a sudden, a hare crossed his path. "Well, well, well, what a pretty rounded hare this is, his coat is like silk, he must be getting on very well," thought Lie-abed. "Where does he go grazing?" and he went in the direction the hare had gone.

After a while he reached a deep ravine and on its bottom — wonder of wonders! — spreading willows grew with high emerald-green grass underneath. He called in people with picks and spades and made them dig there.

It was not long before the diggers struck a strong fountain of crystal clear water. It was so powerful that its stream flowed forth like a river, flooding the whole ravine, and surging like a mighty stream through the parched countryside. People rejoiced and the king gave the man a truly royal reward for having returned moisture to the land.

The happy man could hardly manage to take all the king's gifts with him. So he bought a waggon and a pair of dapple-grey horses, loaded the rare things on it, cracked his whip, and set out for home. And the dapple-grey horses being as quick as sparks, it took no more than three days for him to reach his native village.

He had not been there for many years, so nobody recognized him. Nor could Lie-abed recognize his own house. Everything was spick and span, a new stone lean-to, a fresh birchwood fence, and the barn that had been dilapidated when he left stood like a castle covered with a new shingle roof.

His wife came out to the porch to welcome a young man who had just come back from the field with a scythe slung over his shoulder. The housewife gave the youth such a sweet smile that Lie-abed stood aghast. When she went so far as to embrace and kiss the young man, Lie-abed felt hot blood rush into his head. He seized his whip and raised his arm to strike an awful blow, but at that moment the wood-nymph's last piece of good advice flashed through his head, and he realized that she had always given him good advice. So he dropped the raised arm and turned to the housewife with bitterness.

"Wife, you were well advised to have found yourself a young husbandman, when I left you years ago. I was no use to you anyway."

"Good gracious, my husband, my dear husband," cried the wife, having re-cognized her husband's voice. She put her arms round his neck. "The young husbandman is none other than your own son. He was born to us soon after you left me, twenty years ago."

And so all three of them rejoiced over their happy reunion. Afterwards, they lived in good harmony and prosperity, singing merry songs as they worked, and if they have not died, they are still to be found in that village in the middle of those deep woods.

The Wisdom of Crows

Once an old crow settled on a large island where there was enough food for both people and animals. In early spring she laid three speckled eggs, and when three awfully hungry nestlings were born, the old crow was extremely pleased. All around she had a lot to feed them with, and did not have to fly around so much as she would surely have had to anywhere else.

However, she was not to remain content for long. One night a terrible storm broke out and sea waves flooded the whole island. They were mounting higher and higher until they were level with the nest. The crow was aware that if she was to save her young, she would have to take them far out beyond the sea, but just one and no more was all she could carry.

And so without thinking much she just clutched the first of her young that came her way, and soared from the nest.

When they left the island behind, she said to the young chick, "How will you repay me if I carry you across the sea?"

"I too will carry you about some day, only don't drop me," replied the young chick.

"You lie!" said the old crow angrily, dropped the nestling into the water and returned to the island.

The nest was half flooded already, so she took up her second young and hurried off as fast as her wings would carry her. After a while she asked again, "How will you repay me if I save you?"

"When I grow up, I will carry you anywhere you will want to go."

This time, too, the old crow got angry, and dropped the young chick into the sea.

Then she set out on her journey back to the nest.

It was already flooded, there was just the little head of the last young crow sticking out of the water, and the moment the old crow seized it, the nest disappeared altogether.

Then she flew for a day and a night, and only when she saw the shore with birches on it in the distance she asked for the third time, "How will you repay me, if I save you from drowning?"

"What can I say? When I grow up, I shall have to carry my own young, if need be," answered the young chick after a while.

This time the old crow was satisfied. "You are telling the truth, because birds never look after their parents. Therefore I will carry you as far as the shore, build a new nest, and feed you until you fly out of it by yourself."

The Tale
of the Old Soldier

Being a soldier in the old days was no bed of roses, and a young man who got called up to serve in the army — unless he fell in battle — would come home grey-haired and bent with age.

Mikelis was one of those unfortunates, and when the army finally discharged him, the greater part of his life had been wasted.

In spite of all this, he was in high spirits. Why shouldn't he be? His pouch was full of tobacco, the three ducats he had received for his services were tinkling in his pocket, and there was a knapsack full of good food on his back. He did not mind the sun or the bad weather, just walked on and on following his nose until he saw an old man as frail as a wisp of straw.

The old man begged him for alms, and the veteran promptly gave him one of his golden coins. "Well, why not," he said to himself, "I have two golden coins left, and these will still give me a chance to make a good living."

However, he had not walked even a mile, when once again there was the old man sitting by the road. He again begged the soldier to give him some money, 75 and since the old man was trembling with cold, the soldier presented him with another ducat. "One ducat is enough for me, my uniform and boots are still in order," he comforted himself.

However, he had not reached the next bend yet, and there was the old man again. Already from the distance he lifted his lean hands, and so the good-hearted soldier fished out the last golden coin from his pocket, and handed it to the old man.

"Here you are, and God help you," he said. "You certainly need it, and I can do without any ducats."

At these words the old man smiled gently and said, "You are a good man, Mikelis, and I will reward you for your goodness. Take this," and he handed the soldier an old leather tobacco pouch.

"But I have some tobacco here in my horn, can't you see? I don't need your pouch. Just keep it, it may come in handy."

But the old man shook his head. "This is not an ordinary thing as you may think. If you wish to dispose of your enemies, all you need to say is: 'Hop inside,' and everyone finds himself in the pouch as in prison. So have no hesitation, Mikelis, take it."

"If that is the case, why should I not take it," the old soldier agreed. Then he put the pouch in his pocket, bade the old man farewell, and walked on again.

Before long he came to a royal city. However, already from afar he could see black flags flown from the houses.

"What has befallen you?" he asked the soldier standing guard at the city gate.

The sentry only waved his hand: "We are in a terrible plight. At midnight every day a three-headed devil drives to the castle in his carriage from hell, and always carries off one city maiden. Now it has got so bad that this very night the king has to sacrifice his eldest daughter."

"And no one has stood up to the devil?" said the amazed soldier.

"Many have tried their luck, especially when the king proclaimed he would give half of his kingdom and one of his three daughters in reward to the man who would chase the devil out. But all in vain. Many valiant knights were found dead in the morning. So take my advice — don't enter the city."

However, the veteran said neither this nor that, went through the gate, and set out straight for the castle. To his astonishment there was not a single servant anywhere; the corridors were empty, the windows covered in cobwebs, and only in a remote little chamber the bald-headed king sat upon a dilapidated throne, his head buried in his hands.

He may not have heard the visitor enter, for only after some time did he raise his tearful eyes and say, "What are you doing here? Don't you know what fate awaits you if the devil catches you? You had better run away if you cherish your life."

But Mikelis stood to attention as befits a soldier, and answered in a resolute voice, "I know all this, Your Majesty. And I have come to protect your eldest daughter from the devil at midnight."

The king liked his words. At once he bade his daughters to prepare a rich dinner for the veteran soldier, and when midnight was drawing near, and the soldier happily pulled at his pipe, he said to him, "The devil always arrives at the main entrance. There you must wait for him."

Mikelis nodded, and sending the king and his daughters to bed, he settled in an armchair by the door. Before long the bell started striking midnight in the city. Hardly had the twelfth stroke stopped ringing when a wild noise and neighing was heard on the road to the castle and at that moment a fiery carriage drawn by three black horses pulled up in the courtyard. Then the three-headed devil alighted and shouted gruffly:

"Who is guarding the eldest princess tonight?"

"An old soldier," cried Mikelis undaunted, and himself pulled the door ajar to see what was going to happen next.

However, all at once, the devil was as meek as a lamb. "Since you are an old soldier, I will not disturb your peace. But tomorrow the second princess will be abducted by my six-headed brother. Mind you remember this!"

With these words he cracked his whip over his hellish team, and vanished as quickly as he had appeared. A smell of sulphur was all he left behind.

Well, Mikelis himself was astonished at what an easy time he had on guard-duty, but he did not brood over this for any length of time. He lay back comfortably in his armchair, put out his pipe, and snored happily until the morning.

While the soldier was still sleeping, even after the cocks had crowed in a new day, the king came creeping out of his little chamber to see how things had gone.

He could hardly believe what he saw, and when Mikelis woke and told him everything, the king was so overjoyed that he threw his arms round the old soldier's neck and told him:

"Even now you can claim one half of my kingdom. And if you succeed in chasing away the six-headed devil as well, choose the one of my daughters whom you like best to be your wife."

"I would fancy the youngest," said Mikelis to himself, but what he said aloud was: "The battle is not yet won, Your Majesty, the devils never give up their booty so easily!"

And he was soon to learn that his words had indeed been true. The second day at midnight there was such roar behind the windows that the castle shook in its foundations. And after this a carriage twice as large as the first appeared in the courtyard, drawn by six black horses.

This time even the devil was different, and when he spoke, the windows clattered like mad:

"Who is watching the younger princess tonight?"

"It's me, the old soldier," answered Mikelis courageously, and stepped out of his own accord.

This was something the devil had not expected. At once all the noise subsided, the devil quickly jumped into the carriage, and before he cracked the whip, he just found time to say:

"Today you have won, but wait for tomorrow: My nine-headed brother is coming to carry away the youngest princess!"

Then he and his carriage vanished in the darkness. Mikelis laughed aloud at the devil's flight, and smiled even in his sleep.

The moment he woke up, the king, who was so pleased that rusty hair started growing on his bare head, bestowed even more favour on him than before. The lovely princesses, too, did all they could to please Mikelis and so the old veteran felt as happy as though he were in paradise.

But when midnight was approaching, he realized that his battle was not yet won. Nevertheless, as before he sent both the king and the princesses to bed, and himself sat back in his armchair by the door.

He scarcely heard the midnight bell, but he was blinded and deafened by the thunder and lightning which accompanied the devil's arrival. And then, when everything had died down, the largest carriage that he had ever seen in his life appeared in the courtyard drawn by nine pitch-black stallions.

And then it was the nine-headed Beelzebub himself who alighted from the carriage, rolling his eighteen fiery eyes at the veteran, licking his mouths daintily with his long tongues until simmering sulphur dripped from them to the ground.

"Present yourself, Mikelis, I'll snap you up like a dainty morsel," said the Lord of Devils menacingly, and made straight for the door.

But true to himself, the old soldier never cowered even before the monstrous Lord of Hell. Opening the castle door himself, he stepped out to meet the devil.

"What? Such a midget of a man, and my brothers were scared of him!" The Lord of Hell could not believe his eighteen eyes. "I will make short work of you, you miserable beggar!"

"Mind you don't make a mistake," said the soldier, nothing daunted. "This little pouch is a match for all those teeth, claws and hoofs of yours," he said, pulling out the pouch which the old man had given him.

"Show me," said the devil and curiosity made him jump close to Mikelis.

But that was a thing he ought not to have done. For no sooner had he bent his nine heads over the open pouch than the veteran shouted "Hop inside!" and all of a sudden, the devil shrank till he was no bigger than a mouse, jumped into the pouch, and all Mikelis needed to do was to fasten the string properly. Then he seized his big stick, and beat the dust out of the imprisoned devil's coat with many a heavy blow.

As you can imagine, the nine-headed one yelled, begged for mercy, promised heaven and hell, but the soldier would not leave off till his hand went limp. Indeed, by that time the devil was half dead with pain.

"I will let you go," said Mikelis in the end. "But on one condition."

"I will gladly fulfil every wish of yours, only let me free from this terrible sack," the nine-headed one implored him, and so the soldier did not wait to be asked again:

"Before the cock crows, have so much gold carried into the castle that all the rooms are full up to the ceiling. But mind my words — take care you don't leave out a single little room. Otherwise I won't let you go!"

Willy-nilly the nine-headed one had to yield, and then the soldier experienced something he had never witnessed before in all his life:

From all sides the whole of hell's crew came flying into the castle: devils, hell-hounds, Beelzebubs, Lucifers, old hell's denizens and the young hell's breed, together with their dames and granddames! And each of those evil spirits carried a sack of ducats on his back. There was so much sulphurous dust about that Mikelis had to hold his nose, but the amount of gold growing with every minute was a pleasing sight. And when dawn broke behind the windows, the smallest devil brought the last handful of gold scraped from the bottom of hell. And, at that moment the cock crowed.

"Well, there might still be a little room left for a few more ducats, but for the present I will let you off," said Mikelis magnanimously, untied his magic pouch and let the nine-headed devil out.

You should have seen him flying rocketlike through the window, never to return.

Thus it happened that Mikelis became the richest veteran soldier on earth, but this was not all: Before the week was out, he had received from the old king the promised half of the kingdom, and the youngest and fairest princess became his wife.

It would now seem fitting to add what a happy life Mikelis led after this, and how he reigned as a wise ruler for a long time. However, this was by no means the case. Before the year was out, Death came for Mikelis and carried him off.

The Old Soldier and Death

Thus Mikelis died, but he was rather restless in Heaven. Every now and then he looked down to the Earth to see how his young wife and the old king were faring. Having got a good job in Heaven at the heavenly gate, he had plenty of leisure. But what irked him most was that down below in the castle he had left behind his magic pouch, and he was anxious that it should not get into wrong hands.

However, no person who had once got to Heaven could return to the Earth. Only hardened sinners were being sent by God straight to Hell. But the old soldier did not fancy the idea of going there — as we know, he had quite a few things to answer for in the devil's domain.

And so Mikelis kept watch over the heavenly gate, now and then letting in a few good souls with whom he had a chat about the world, but most of the time he badly missed the Earth.

One day Godmother Death herself came to knock at Heaven's gate with her bony hand. "Whatever do you want?" asked Mikelis, looking out of his lodge.

"I have come to ask the Lord to give me some work to do," answered Death clanking menacingly with her scythe.

Mikelis hated the look of that gaunt old woman, so he said, "Wait here, we don't let such apparitions enter Heaven. I will go and ask myself."

And so he went. The Heavenly Father was just combing his very long white beard with a gold comb, and when the old soldier told him of Death's request, he just said casually, "Well, if she has nothing to do, let her mow down old people on Earth for three years."

Truth to tell, this was something Mikelis in no way approved of. For Death could come and carry off his father-in-law, the old king, and who would then take care of the kingdom and the princesses?

"He said you should eat the bark off old oaks for three years." He gave Godmother Death the message as if it were God's truth, and banged the gate shut before her bony nostrils.

Three years passed, and Death appeared in Heaven once again. The bones on her were rattling like mad, and only teeth were to be seen under the ragged headcloth.

"Fie, what a fright you have given me," spat Mikelis when he looked out of the lodge. "What is it you want now?"

"I have gnawed off all the bark from old oaks, and did not fancy it at all. I want some better work to do."

"Well, wait here, and I will go and arrange it for you," said Mikelis and hastened to report to the Lord: "Death wants you to know that she has already mowed down all the old people and has nothing to do."

The Lord looked up from his white beard, for again he was combing it with his gold comb, and said, "So let her mow down the young, they are more numerous."

"No fear," said Mikelis to himself. "The ugly old hag might carry off my lovely princess." And so he gave the godmother the following message:

"The Lord says you should gnaw off young oak trees for a change. But take my advice, you had better not come here any more, my master thinks you are not doing your job properly."

"Alas and wellaway," lamented Death. "My job is to mow down people, and not to gnaw the bark off trees. Just look how feeble I have become! And now it is young oaks, which are even worse than old."

"You don't look a picture of health, I must say," said the soldier pretending to agree. "So follow my advice, and don't come here any more, or you will have to gnaw at stones."

Death did not wait to hear any more. She seized her scythe and hurried off to the woods lest the Lord should change his mind and really order her to gnaw at stones. But Mikelis roared with laughter until his lodge shook.

Thereupon, as often happens, he forgot all about Death, and when exactly three years had passed and she appeared, he was fast asleep at his post.

And so Death slipped past Mikelis unobserved, and went straight to see the Lord. She really was so haggard you could have bound her in a small bundle, her teeth all shaky, her bones ready to fall to pieces.

The Lord got such a fright he would have preferred to run away from her, but Death stood in his way.

"All these six years I had been gnawing at trees as Mikelis said you ordered me. However, you know only too well what my real job is in the world. So at last give me the work which properly belongs to me!"

"So, it was Mikelis," the Lord interrupted the godmother's stream of words. "Now go and pick people at will. Mikelis has outwitted you but have no fear, he shall be taught a lesson."

So Death had to make do with God's promise, though she would have preferred to settle accounts with the soldier herself. "I hope he will not try to pull a fast one on me next time," she said menacingly, and hurried off to Earth.

Mikelis was still happily asleep when the ruler of Heaven shook him roughly to give him a piece of his mind. "So this is how you do your duty at the gate! I should send you straight to Lucifer for having hoaxed Godmother Death."

The old soldier knew at once what must have happened, and so he put on his sorriest face and never said a word.

That made the Lord take pity on him so that he finally decided, "For punishment I will send you back to the Earth so that you can mend your ways there and learn to think highly of your duty at the heavenly gate."

What more could Mikelis wish for? Though he still put on a very sorry face, this was only so as not to show his pleasure right away, nor later when two angels carried him right down to his castle.

Only when he set eyes on the princess and the old king again did he show his delight. He had barrels of beer and wine rolled out into the royal courtyard, the cooks received orders to cook, fry or bake the best dishes, and then everybody in and below the castle had a good time eating, drinking, and feasting.

However, after a week of merrymaking there came a disastrous report: Godmother Death has appeared in the city! She went about in the square and in the streets, and whoever she picked was sent to his grave by her scythe.

Finally she set out for the castle. By that time the roads were empty as though freshly swept, and so the godmother had to spend some time looking about for the next victim.

And lo and behold: Mikelis himself was walking in her direction, with no weapon on him. The only thing he pressed in his hands was a small leather pouch, and he was smiling at Godmother Death as if he had no care in the world.

"Now you're for it, you shall soon stop smiling," croaked Death, and jumping to the soldier's side waved her scythe.

But Mikelis was quicker than she; he opened the leather pouch and cried: "Hop inside!" and before the blade could even touch him, Death and her scythe were imprisoned inside.

She tossed about for all she was worth, cried, called him names, but it all availed her nothing. Mikelis had tied the pouch properly, and making sure there was no one to watch him, he ran up to the top floor of the castle tower, where he put it inside an old chest. Just to make sure, he locked it with nine turns of the lock.

In order not to lose the key of the chest he hung it round his neck, and went off merrily to ascend the throne.

He reigned with justice and wisdom for so many years that he managed to

bring up a dozen sons, followed by grandsons, great grandsons and great great grandsons.

In the end, however, he realized it was time to hand over the royal crown to his eldest son, for he suddenly missed his sentry duty at the gate.

But who would be willing to let a famous king serve as an ordinary sentry? In vain did old Mikelis implore, in vain did he even offer the soldiers in the castle to take over their duty if only for a little while. Instead of obliging their king, they all said such work was unsuited for him.

And so in the end the inevitable happened. Mikelis came to recall his post at the heavenly gate and how the Lord must be missing him there. So one night before daybreak he hobbled up to the tower again after so many years, opened the old chest, and opened the pouch where Godmother Death was already waiting for him . . .

The Quarrelsome Brothers

Once upon a time there was a hard-working husbandman in a village. The farm flourished in his hands. But all of a sudden a misfortune befell him — his wife died leaving behind four children: three well-built sons, good but rather quarrelsome, and little Magdalen, as gentle as a flower.

The farmer mourned for his wife for a long time, but in the end he married again. What else was he to do? The farm needed a housekeeper, the children needed a mother. But he was not lucky in the good-looking woman he chose. He had no inkling she was an evil witch.

One Sunday, the farmer was getting ready to go to town to visit his relatives and show them his new wife. The sons pulled out the carriage from the shed, and gave it a fine polish. When they were about to put horses to the carriage, they could not agree on whether white horses or black ones were better suited for that festive occasion.

The quarrel was so fierce that the husbandman himself had to choose; he decided in favour of black horses. However, that was not the end of the quarrel. The brothers went on quarrelling and calling each other names; it was a wonder they did not fall to blows.

It was at this point that the stepmother intervened. "I can see, lads, that you find pleasure in quarrelling, and I am sure you are eager to fight one another. So your wish shall come true: you shall quarrel and fight among yourselves as long as you live, but not here. You must go away."

No sooner had the stepmother uttered her curse than she waved a white wand towards the gate. The gate opened of itself and the brothers, still quarrelling and jogging one another, ran out into the street.

Their father laughed aloud at his sons, then cracked his whip over the horses and, unconcerned, drove off on a visit to the town with his wife.

However, the lads never came back home that day. Nor did they come back the next day, and they were not seen in the neighbourhood ever again. The earth seemed to have swallowed them up.

This was most saddening for Magdalen, their little sister. She missed her brothers and, with tears in her eyes, looked for them everywhere. The father's face, too, became furrowed with deep wrinkles. However, the stepmother strutted about like a peacock. She made the girl do the worst jobs, and when she lost her temper, shut her up and starved her in the cellar the whole day.

No wonder the poor little girl could not stand the way she was treated at home. One day she tied her poor belongings into a bundle and set out into the world to seek her brothers.

She walked on and on wherever her eyes would lead her, through forests, across fields and meadows, waded through brooks and rivers, skirted lakes, climbed mountain ridges until she came to a rock which blocked her way.

She knocked on the stone wall, the rock opened, and the maiden found herself on the threshold of a blue cave. An old man rose from the hearth and said, "Come on in, Little Maud. You must be tired after your travels. Come and sit down, but not on this chair. Better sit down on the fur in front of the fireplace and tell me about your worries."

Maud told the old man all about her brothers whom the witch of a step-mother had enchanted into constant quarrelling and driven away from home.

"I have no idea where your brothers might be. I have never heard of them. But I will ask the animals if they have seen them."

They stepped out on the threshold of the cave, the old man pulled out a willow whistle from his sleeve and whistled a pretty tune. All at once, animals, great and small, came running together. The old man asked them if they had not seen three young men who kept quarrelling, but none of the animals knew anything about them.

Little Maud was sad, but the old man consoled her: "Do not despair, little maiden, we will ask the birds now. They fly beyond our horizons, and might know something about your brothers."

And so they did.

The old man called together all the birds with his whistle, and a sparrow-hawk recalled that on the southern side of the Green Lake he had seen three young men pounding one another with iron rods till the ringing resounded far and wide.

The very next day the maiden got ready to set out in search of her brothers. When they parted the old man gave her a willow whistle and a pair of leather boots.

"Those are no ordinary boots," he said. "They will lead you to the Green Lake by themselves. They have soles of iron, and when you have worn them down, you will be close to your journey's end. And the whistle will help your brothers to get rid of their quarrelsome habits. Once they blow it, they will never again quarrel. But remember, each must play it of his own free will, you must neither force nor persuade them to do so. If you did, the whistle would lose its magic power."

Little Maud gratefully kissed the old man's hand, hid the magic whistle in her bundle, put on her magic shoes, and set out on her further pilgrimage.

And again she walked across forests, fields and meadows, crossed brooks and rivers, climbed steep mountain ridges, until one day she felt a little stone stick into her boot. She took it off to knock it out, and all at once she saw that her iron sole was all worn through, full of holes.

Little Maud recalled the old man's words, and her heart jumped with joy. She was near the end of her travels at last.

And indeed, that very evening she did reach the Green Lake. A stone house stood on the high shore. She looked into the lighted window, and in the large room saw her brothers having their dinner in good cheer around the table.

She knocked and entered the room. It was a strange meeting. Her brothers did not recognize her, nor did she disclose to them who she was. She asked to be allowed to stay the night.

The young men were surprised, but they did not refuse to put her up for the night. Only they warned her not to take fright in the morning when she heard a lot of din and ringing of iron.

"When the sun climbs over the lake in the morning," the eldest brother explained to her, "then our time comes, and we are bound to fight until sunset. That is the curse uttered by our witch of a stepmother because at home we used to fight all the time. But don't be afraid, we shall not harm one another. For we are brothers born, and fond of each other!"

And indeed, in the morning the maiden was awakened by a terrible din and a clashing sound. She looked out of the window, and was in a cold sweat all at once. For on the shore of the Green Lake her brothers were fighting. They attacked one another with long iron rods, and ugly words.

The maiden quickly shut the window and set about putting the house in order. Anything but to have not to watch her brothers at one another's throats.

Then she made a fire in the oven, made dough for bread in the kneading-trough, and set about baking. She made three loaves: a smaller one well sprinkled with cummin, and a bigger loaf for the middle one in which she buried her golden ring, an heirloom from her mother. For the eldest brother she baked a big loaf of bread with the magic whistle hidden inside it.

When the sun had set, the brothers returned home all boisterous after the fighting. They were contented and engaged in a friendly conversation. It was a pleasant surprise for them to find the room all tidied up and to breathe the smell of freshly baked bread. The youngest impatiently cut a crackling first crust from the gold-coloured loaf, and bit into it with great gusto.

"This is the kind of bread that only our mother could bake," he said with his mouth full.

The other two also fell to and ate their loaves; the smell of the bread had reminded them of their distant home.

When the middle one was cutting himself a slice, his knife slid over something round. He buried the point in the crumb, and retrieved a ring with a red stone.

"Just look, boys, what I have found!" he cried in astonishment.

The youngest inspected the gold ring, and suddenly exclaimed, "Good gracious, it is the ring of our late mother! How did it ever get inside there? For it was our little sister that mother gave it to on her deathbed."

"Where the ring is, there must be our little Maud," decided the eldest brother and at once started looking for the girl who had come to their cottage unexpectedly the night before. At this the little sister, hidden behind the oven and no longer able to contain herself, ran out to meet her brothers. She laughed and cried for sheer joy, embraced them and told them how sad things were at home, how long she had had to wander through the world before she found them, and how happy she was to see them all together again.

The brothers too were moved by the unexpected reunion, but when little Maud used the words "come back", all of them became sorry and sad, and the eldest said, "We just can't go back among men, people would laugh at us. And you can't stay here either."

"Why not?"

"Well, you saw it yourself this morning! The moment the sun rises, we can't help fighting each other, and then we are beyond ourselves with fury. You yourself might come to harm at the hands of one of us, and that would be the end of us, for then we would kill one another. And you surely don't want that to happen!" said the eldest, and he cut into the loaf. But his knife struck against something hard. He moved it about a little in the crust, until he pulled out the willow whistle.

Amazed, he turned to his brothers. "What can this mean?"

"Well, what can it be? Can't you see it is a willow whistle? We made many a one like that when we were boys. Remember?" said the middle one, and reached out for the whistle. "Let me have it for a while! I will whistle something. I hope I haven't forgotten how to blow it."

Then he put the whistle to his lips, and blew gently. What they heard were the sweet tones of a lullaby.

The brothers stopped eating.

"This is the song mother used to sing us when we were little boys," said the eldest, and turned to the middle one. "Please let me have the whistle for a while, I would like to play it a little myself."

He put the whistle to his lips, his fingers dancing about lightly upon it, and at that moment the melancholy melody of an old song from their home could be heard. They all listened, and suddenly they had such a fine feeling, but a little sad, too.

"Give me that pipe, or you will make us all cry!" said the youngest after a while, got hold of the whistle, and the moment he blew into it, it burst into a merry tripping tune.

When the young men heard the frolicsome tune, at once their sadness left them. They grabbed Maud and started dancing.

The maiden was happy, since all her brothers had played on the whistle of their own accord. Everything was set for the prophecy of the old man from the blue cave to come true: All the three of them should be freed from that frightful curse now.

And they were!

In the morning the sun had risen over the horizon and the brothers never even thought of getting ready for their fight. In peace and harmony they had their breakfast. Their sister made a point of fetching their iron rods for them, but they had no idea what to do with them. All their squabbles and quarrellings of the day before were forgotten. And that was a good thing.

After lunch they locked up the house, and set out for home. Suddenly they were all homesick for their native village.

This time they went merrily along, but they had to walk through woods and fields, wade across brooks and rivers, cross mountain ridges, until once again they reached the rock, which had blocked their passage.

Little Maud knocked on the stone wall, the rock opened, and the old man gave them a hearty welcome. "Just step inside, dear friends. I can see, dear maiden, you have done well: you have found your brothers, and now you are bringing them home with you, aren't you?"

Maud returned to the old man the willow whistle which had freed her brothers from their evil enchantment, and thanked him from the bottom of her heart. The old man was pleased with her gratitude. He looked round the blue cave for something to give the young people to make them happy. Then he took his only chair and handed it to the brothers.

"As a souvenir I give you this larch chair, but take care never to sit on it. Whoever sits on it shall never rise again. But it will be of good service to you. Just take one leg each and it will take you wherever you order it to go. So best of luck to you, friends." He bade them farewell and saw them out to the road in front of the rock.

At once the brothers and their sister took hold of one leg each, and expressed their wish: "Home, home!"

The chair rose high right up to the clouds, and then, like a strange bird, quickly set course for their native village.

They were overjoyed to see again their old father, who suddenly became much younger when he saw all his children around him.

Of course, the stepmother at once took a perch on the beautiful larch chair — but that was her undoing — immediately she lost all her magic power, and

never rose from the chair again. First she begged for help, crying and giving all sorts of promises, then she cursed everybody and in the end she called upon thunder and lightning and all devils to come to her aid.

And the devils did come flying there, and carried her off, along with the chair, to hell.

After a time, the brothers got married, and so did little Maud, and then they all lived happily in their village until they died. Now it is their children's children who live and work there. They are all doing well, even more than well, and they never quarrel.

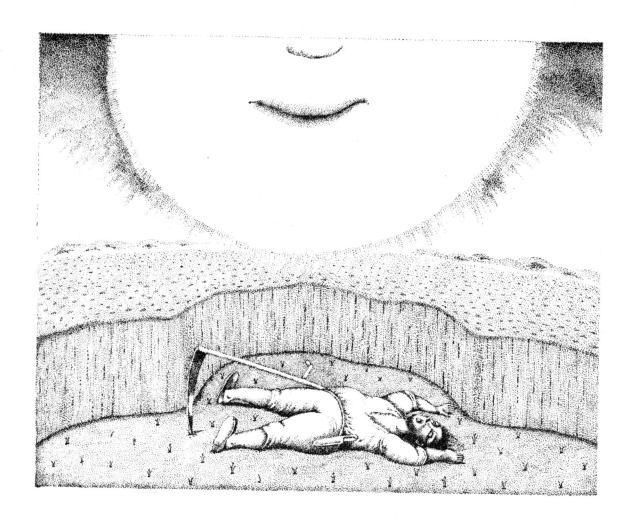

The Sun, the Frost and the Wind

Anything, absolutely anything, can occur in a fairy tale. Thus, once upon a time the Sun, the Frost and the Wind happened to be walking together along a road. They got to talking, and before long fell arguing about who was the strongest creature in the world.

The Sun said, "I am generally esteemed for the light and warmth I give off. But I can also burn, and then everybody is struck with awe. So I am the strongest of all."

"Oh, do not brag," rejoined the Frost quickly. "What power do you possess in winter? In that season everyone is afraid of me, let me tell you. I am the strongest of all."

Thus the two went on arguing trying to outstrip each other. Only the Wind did not say a word, but just listened to them carefully.

Before long they met a poor peasant who was just returning from the town. The moment he spotted the pilgrims he took off his cap and made a low bow to them.

"You see," said the Sun when the peasant had passed them. "He bowed to me, since I am the strongest."

The Frost laughed scornfully. "Go away with your pretensions. That bow was definitely meant for me. Didn't you notice how frightened that man looked?"

And the two would have been sure to fall out again had not the Wind hit upon a good idea.

"Hey, little man," he shouted after the departing peasant; and when the peasant, though none too willingly, returned, the Wind asked him:

"Which of us did you actually bow to? The Sun, the Frost or myself?"

The peasant looked from one to the other: the Frost was frowning morosely, the Sun, though he wore a kindly smile on his face, seemed to have embers for eyes. The Wind was wafting lightly, gently blowing down the road, softening the cold issuing from the Frost, but also cooling the heat radiated by the Sun.

"Indeed, it was you, kind Wind, I made my bow to," said the peasant without pausing to think.

Well, neither the Frost nor the Sun found this a pleasant answer.

"You shall get to know yet how strong we are!" they yelled at the poor peasant angrily, and before you could say Jack Robinson, the Sun was up in the sky and hidden behind the clouds, while the Frost was dashing away as far as the forest which darkened the horizon.

Only the Wind remained with the peasant and said, "Have no fear, and go home in peace. But, should either of the two try to harm you, just call on me to come and help you. I am more than a match for them."

With these words the Wind blew off on his way, and the peasant set out for home.

He might have forgotten all about it, but that year winter set in very early, and there was a cruel biting frost. The peasant did not dare even to go out into the courtyard for fear his nose might freeze and drop off. The wood in the cottage was nearly used up. On the day he burnt the last piece, the Frost came into his room.

"I have come to show you who is the strongest!" he shouted rattling the door.

The peasant's blood froze in his veins with horror and cold, as the Frost stuck his icy claws into the cabin. At the last moment the man thought of the Wind and begged him:

"Wind, oh Wind, dear friend,
Come and give your helping hand.
The Frost is cold and cruel,
Hurry please and bring your fuel."

And lo! Only once or twice more did the Frost rattle the door, before he began to sigh and moan himself. The icicles on his beard started thawing and in the end he fled to the woods. Thereupon a soft warm breeze blew in through the door, which was standing ajar, and the peasant once again felt blood flowing in his veins.

After that, the Frost never appeared anywhere near the peasant's house, and before long the peasant forgot all about him.

Spring passed and summer set in. There was always plenty of work to do in the fields and meadows, and every evening the peasant would come home late, all tired and done in by the heat.

One day at midday he was making hay. The Sun had been burning since the morning, but now the peasant had a feeling that it was sinking lower and lower in the sky and was about to burn him to cinders. In despair he dropped the rake, and pressing himself down to the earth, cried out:

> *"Wind, oh Wind, dear friend,*
> *If a moment you do tarry,*
> *The Sun will burn me in a hurry,*
> *And that will be my end!"*

And just as the peasant was about to faint, he felt a cooling breeze on his cheek. Though the Sun worked hard, his rays lost all their strength. The peasant rose, picked up his rake and set to work again with a will.

After that time the Sun and the Frost never tried to do him harm. And the peasant congratulated himself on having correctly adjudged the greatest strength to the Wind when the three of them just could not agree.

There is no Man Like the Blacksmith

Once upon a time a cotter and his wife lived happily together in a village. They had three daughters. Then, after many years, a son was born to them. The parents' joy knew no bounds.

From the very cradle little Jurgis was their pampered darling child. He always got everything he wanted, and whatever he felt like doing, that he was allowed to do.

The mother was particularly fond of her dear little son, and when he had grown up a little, she made him a feather-bed on top of the oven, and even brought food to him there so that he would not have to get up.

No wonder then that as time went on the beloved little boy turned into a sluggard. He was waited upon by everyone, so all he did was to lie abed on the oven, never doing a spot of work himself, and tyrannizing the others.

The father was the first to worry about his dear son. "Mother, I fear," he said one day, "that boy of ours will come to no good end. Look, he is beginning to have a beard, and is still doing nothing. He has no trade, and is fed like a fledgling in a nest, the good-for-nothing."

"Let him be, our sweet little darling," the mother replied. "He will have enough toil in life after we are gone."

"That's just the problem. What will become of him when we die? He will remain a burden on his sisters' neck. He doesn't even know how to make fire in the stove, the lazy beggar," complained the father bitterly, and he was right.

One day, having returned from the field, the father gave his son a searching look and said, "Come down, you stay-at-home, we will have a talk together."

"There is no need to get up for a bit of talk," rejoined Jurgis lazily, but when he saw his father get hold of the poker, he slid down from the oven promptly enough.

"Well, well, there is no need to take life so seriously," he mumbled sleepily.

"No need to take it seriously now, but there will be when we are here no longer," said the father. "For there is nothing you are good at. Your mother cooks your meals and feeds you, your sisters do your washing and the chores, and all you do is to wallow about in the feather-bed, and you hardly ever even wash yourself. Just look how filthy you are! There is yesterday's semolina still on your chin! You shall go and learn some trade so that you can earn your living like a decent man, and not be a burden on anyone. You are strong enough to break stones. You shall go and serve as an apprentice."

"Why not?" yawned Jurgis. "I will go when it can't be helped. I am beginning to feel bored at home anyway; it is awfully dull. But what trade should I learn?"

"What about bricklaying?" suggested the father. "There is a lot of building going on everywhere, you would earn a lot of money."

"No, I will not be a bricklayer," rejoined the son. "To be working on scaffolding all the time. I might even fall down, and in winter my hands would get frost-bitten."

"So go and become a tailor. In that case you'll be working in a warm room all the time."

"A tailor — no fear!" laughed Jurgis. "He sits for days on end huddled up over his material. That is not a healthy job. Before long my back would be bent and my fingers all pricked with needles."

"And what about becoming a blacksmith?" suggested the father. "Wouldn't you like that? That is indeed a trade for a real man: fire, iron, hammer and anvil."

"Yes, blacksmith's work is something I might fancy," admitted the son, and that decided it.

The very next day, the father took Jurgis to a distant town to apprentice him to a fine blacksmith. He paid the man five gold ducats in advance for his son's apprenticeship, and said to his son as he bid him farewell, "Watch everything carefully, and never let your eyes wander off your master, so that you may learn a lot in the three years!"

The first day Jurgis looked for an oven in the smithy where he could lie, but there was no oven there.

However, a mother's heart can see things even at a distance. And so the very next day secretly, without his father's knowledge, she brought him a bed, placed it in a corner in the smithy, and piled it high with pillows so that her dear son might rest in a soft bed after his long day's toil.

But the dear boy did not wait till the evening. No sooner was his mother gone than he crept inside the feather-bed. When his master allotted him some work, he excused himself by saying he was tired, and that his father had told him anyway just to watch carefully, as the surest way towards learning a great deal.

Several times more the master bade the sluggard do some work, but seeing it was in vain, he just waved his hand, stopped bothering about him, and never took any notice of him again.

And so for three years Jurgis lay in his bed in the smithy. When he felt like it, he watched his master at work, but when the powerful blows on the anvil rang out, he preferred to hide his head under the pillow so as not to go deaf from the noise.

Three years passed, and the father came to fetch his son and take him home. "Well, master, has our boy acquired something of your blacksmith's art during these years?" inquired the father.

"Well, he did watch me, but what he learnt and if you are going to be satisfied, that I can hardly say," replied the blacksmith vaguely.

At home the father had turned a little old barn into a smithy for his son. He had bought a new anvil, a pretty bellows, a couple of blacksmith's sledge-hammers and several pairs of tongs. At once he took his son there, put a piece of iron in the fireplace for him, and pulling the bellows himself, he said, "Well, show me what you have learnt. Go and hammer a new share to my plough."

The son tucked up his shirt sleeves, put on a heavy leather apron and set to work. He hammered away like mad, with pieces of red-hot iron flying off in all directions, until there was only a small piece left on the anvil.

"What will a new ploughshare be good for?" he said turning to his father after a while. "The old one is still good enough and will last you a long time yet. I will hammer out a new axe for you, shall I?"

"All right," agreed the father. "I do need a new axe, the old one is blunt now."

And again Jurgis hammered at the iron until splinters flew off in all directions. In the end, only a very small piece was left on the anvil for him to work.

"Now this is not enough to hammer an axe out of," murmured the son. "But father, I will make quite a few nice nails out of this for you."

"Well, why not, nails are always useful to have about the house," said the father resignedly.

So Jurgis set to hammering out nails, but once again his work did not prosper. One nail was too thin, the other too thick, the third was crooked, the fourth without a head — well, one worse than the other, nothing but rejects and spoiled work.

"And what will you make now out of the scrap, son?" asked the father.

"I will hammer out a few needles," decided the young blacksmith.

"Well, do if you can, your mother will be pleased," said the father with a frown.

The son set about hammering once again, but it was no good. The needles were square, crooked, had neither eyes nor points.

Jurgis threw the hammer into the corner, threw his work into a bucket, and growled angrily:

"The iron was poor, one couldn't make anything out of it."

"The iron was good, and it's you who can't make anything. Badly you have learnt your trade. An idler and good-for-nothing, that's what you are! I am not going to provide for you any more. Get out of my sight, and don't come back till you have become a proper hard-working man!" said the father showing his lazy son the door.

The mother cried and begged her husband to show pity on her dear son, but the man was firm this time, and the ne'er-do-well boy was driven out.

So Jurgis went. He passed through villages and towns. Here he got a slice of bread, there a boiled potato, or a cup of milk. At one house, he was taken to task by the housekeeper:

"Such a sturdy young man, and you aren't ashamed of begging. You're none too fond of work, are you?"

Jurgis felt ashamed and quickly left the village. He got as far as the edge of the forest, and there he sat down; he leaned against a tree-stump, and for the first time in his life pondered about what he should really do. He did not feel in the least like laughing.

There were cows grazing about and chewing the cud in contented ease. He envied them their lot.

Suddenly, he heard queer buzzing and moaning sounds, as if a thousand very thin voices were moaning and complaining

Looking round he saw a large ant-hill all ruined behind the stump against which he was leaning. Probably some cow had wandered in those parts and trodden the sophisticated structure underfoot.

"Oh you poor little things." The young man felt sorry for the ants who were swarming in the ruins of their home.

Then on a low little knoll he saw a big black ant who was issuing various orders to all the others in his thin sharp voice: "The lower squad shall take care of the wounded. The higher squad shall transfer the eggs underground, the third platoon shall remove obstacles and free the roads, the military group shall mount sentries, ensure work security, and give alarm at once should the four-legged foe draw near again."

Like well-drilled soldiers the ants quickly formed ranks and files, and the salvage work began. The ruins of the ant-hill gradually disappeared and were replaced by new corridors, walls, bridges and little terraces. The enthusiasm with which the ants were rebuilding their destroyed home held Jurgis spellbound. He resolved to help the busy little workers.

From the ruins he picked the big stones, which had been heaped up by the cow's hoofs, and raked up the pine-needles and the moss which had rolled nearly down to the path. Finally, he drove some piles into the earth around the ant-hill, and made a little fence so that cows might never again cause such a terrible catastrophe.

When he was finished, and contemplating the great construction work from a stump, a large red ant climbed along his leg up to his lap, and said in a thin sharp voice:

"You are a good man, Jurgis. You've helped us a lot with the rebuilding of our home. But for your clever hands, we would never have managed to repair the damage so quickly. Should you ever need help in your work, you only have to whistle three times, and we shall be happy to come. You've seen what quick workers we are."

"That I have, indeed, and I will never forget it," said the young man and the red ant went his way again.

Jurgis stayed sitting on the stump for a while, deep in thought. Then he suddenly decided he would go back to the master blacksmith to learn the trade properly. And he actually did what he had resolved to do.

The blacksmith was none too glad to see Jurgis again, but he did not refuse to take him on. This time, it was a different apprenticeship. He never let the young man off from any work, making him cope with the hardest tasks, and run quickly from one job to another. It was a wonder that the sledge-hammer did not grow fast onto Jurgis's hands. A year passed, and Jurgis had become a real blacksmith's journeyman. No kind of work was too hard, everything was child's play for him.

The master was extremely pleased with his new journeyman's performance, and reluctant to let him go; yet he felt he must. But Jurgis said to him earnestly, "Master, for many years I gave you nothing but trouble. I would be glad to work for you for some time yet."

The master was happy looking forward to the clever journeyman being a real help to him in future. And he never came to regret it.

One day a noble knight jumped off his horse in front of the smithy. He was returning from a crusade. His armour was heavily marked with the traces of fighting: a bent chest plate on his mail-coat, his helmet split in two, his sword broken, his shield pierced, and his spear forked and with no point left.

The knight spoke roughly to the blacksmith, saying that he must have all of his armour repaired and a new sword hammered out by morning. If he did manage it overnight, he would give him twenty ducats in gold; if not, his smithy would be burnt down.

The blacksmith was scared out of his wits by the knight's arrogant words. At once he started stammering excuses — he, the blacksmith, could never manage that, it being the work for a tinsmith, a silversmith and an armourer; even if he had ten journeymen, they would never manage to put everything in order by morning anyway.

"But we shall, master, we shall manage to do it overnight. You may rely on it, noble knight," declared Jurgis calmly, and immediately ran off to the smithy.

The blacksmith was so amazed by his journeyman's bold words that he was left speechless.

Thereupon the crusader trotted off, and the blacksmiths got down to work. Even before evening fell, they had a sword hammered out of best steel and sharpened. Then Jurgis told his master to go to bed, and assured him he would finish all the rest by morning on his own.

It was no easy work, however: the chest plate was so badly bent that he had to spend nearly all night hammering it out bit by bit. Dawn was nearly breaking when he started work on the helmet, and there were the shield and the spear still left to do. How was the poor young man to manage all this by morning?

All of a sudden, the unhappy Jurgis thought of the ants and whistled three times. In a moment they were with him. One squad after the other, platoon after platoon, the little workers marched into the smithy, and the red ant immediately allotted them their respective tasks. Some worked the bellows and kept the fire burning, the second group — and these made up the majority — had little hammers and were using these to hammer out the new helmet, another squad was riveting the broken shield. Jurgis got hold of the split spear, exchanged the ashwood shafts and hammered out a sharp point to put on top.

By the time the first cock crowed, everything was ready. Jurgis said goodbye to the ants thanking them many times for having helped him so readily. Then he sat down in the doorway of the smithy and fell asleep. The poor young man had been through a really hard night.

The blacksmith did not have a good night's rest either. He kept waking up; and when he heard the cocks crow, he started and ran to the workshop impatiently. When he saw the sleeping journeyman in the doorway, he shook him violently and yelled, "You unfortunate man, you are happily sleeping here like a newborn babe, and the crusader is going to set fire to the roof over our heads in a moment!"

"Have no fear, master," said the journeyman rubbing his eyes. "Everything is ready, just have a look round!"

And so it was. In the grey light of the smithy the knight's repaired armour was shining as if it were of pure gold.

The master closely inspected one piece after another, and then he nodded his head in recognition. "You are a brick, my boy. You know the blacksmith's trade like a real master. I cannot keep you back here any more. Your father has already made a workshop ready for you at home long ago."

Jurgis was pleased with his master's words, and, moreover, he had been homesick for a long time.

Even before breakfast-time the crusader came up riding on his steed. He was surprised to see his armour in perfect order again. He was so pleased that he even paid the blacksmith five ducats more than had been agreed. Then he put on his armour, set the helmet on his head, fastened the sword to his side, weighed the spear in his hand, and rode off to fight another battle.

The blacksmith wanted to share the gold ducats with his journeyman, but Jurgis would not take any. He asked for a different kind of reward: "I will go back home and I should like to bring some presents for my people. Master, let me have a piece of iron, and I will hammer out some nice things for them. When they see what I have learnt from you, they will truly be overjoyed to see me back."

The master agreed and picked a really big piece of the best metal he had in the workshop for Jurgis to work. During the day the lad was working for the master, and long into the night he was preparing the gifts for his parents and sisters.

For his mother he hammered out a decorative little chest, in which he deposited a set of pins and needles hammered out of the finest steel. For one sister he made an ornamental frame for her looking glass, for his second sister he devised he comb on which he engraved a cabbage-rose, for the third he hammered out a special clasp in the shape of a butterfly.

The present for his father was the last he made, a richly decorated goblet.

When he had all his presents ready, he put them in a basket, bade farewell to the master blacksmith and set out for home.

At home, they were all overjoyed to see Jurgis again, the mother being more pleased than anybody else. When he started handing out his presents, they were all astonished at the beauty of Jurgis's work.

To celebrate his son's return the father poured out some wine for everybody, using his new goblet for his, and said:

"May I propose a toast, my son, to honour our reunion and your skilful hands. I can see there is no man like the blacksmith."

And so they all made merry until late into the night. But the next day from early morning hard blows were heard coming from the anvil in the new smithy, and clusters of sparks were flying off even outside the place.

Before midday there was the first horse standing in front of the smithy, come to get a new horseshoe.

And the horseshoe, as you know, always brings luck.

The Spider and the Fly

This happened far back in the ancient days when men did not know fire and lived in the dark, ate raw meat, and went about wrapped up in furs all the year round, because they were cold and there was nothing to make them warm.

The never-ending winter and dreary darkness were getting irksome even for the noble lords and ladies in the royal castle. And it was then that the wise ruler proclaimed he would pay a high reward of a thousand ducats in gold to anybody who could bring fire from the chasm of Hell.

In those days the king was an almighty sovereign in his country. Not only men but all living creatures had to obey and worship him. When the king was walking abroad, all people went down on their knees before him, all animals crawled silently in the dust by the road, birds stopped in their flight, and all bees and bumble-bees ceased buzzing, so highly they esteemed their king.

The announced reward proved very tempting for many men. Many a brave young swain attempted to bring fire to the king, but each found his doom in the abyss of Hell. Some animals — the clever fox, the daring lynx and the swift-footed elk — set out in search of fire, but they never returned. The eagle also tried to grasp fire in his strong claws, but he scorched his wings and fell to his death in the flames. In vain did the king and his people wait for fire. No one dared any more to climb down into Hell's chasm.

It was then that a clever courtier came forward with the following advice: "Your Majesty, you must increase the reward. You should proclaim that whoever brings fire will be allowed to sit and eat at the same table with you. That is an honour that no one will want to miss."

The king did not fancy the idea very much. Why should he sit at the royal table with anybody? In the end he rather changed the appeal and thereupon messengers proclaimed in every quarter of his realm that anyone who brings fire, be he man, beast or insect, will be allowed to sit at any table ever after.

Once again, many men and beasts endeavoured to fetch fire from the gorge of Hell, but all in vain — none succeeded.

The spider never breathed a word to anyone and began spinning a very very long rope. For three days and three nights he worked before he was ready. Then he casually tied one end of the rope round a boulder at the edge of the abyss, and quickly began his descent into the pit of Hell. He was in a hurry — no one must get there before him. But who could outstrip the spider, the experienced mountaineer? In seven hours he descended to the very bottom of the pit, seized a bit of fire, and slowly started his journey up again. It took him another seven hours before he climbed up to the earth holding the fire. But he was so tired that he could hardly keep his eyes open:

"I will take a nap, there is no hurry. It is dark anyway, and in the morning I will take the fire to the king. He will be pleased, and I shall become the richest creature under the sun!" mused the spider reasonably. He hid the fire between two stones, stretched his little legs exhausted with the climbing, and fell fast asleep. Tired as he was he slept all night, not even the sun woke him.

That morning a fly happened to be flying past. She smelled the smoke, and wondered where it might be coming from. After a while she discovered the sleeping spider, and lifting the two stones, saw the fire between them. Oh, what a rare thing to see! Silently she picked up the fire, and flew with it straight to the king.

There was no end of rejoicing. All people were happy and shouted with enthusiasm:

"We have fire! We have warmth! Long live the king! Long live the one who has brought the fire!" At once the king had a scroll made out for the fly and confirmed it with three seals, and what the scroll said was that the fly and all her progeny, both present and future, might from that day forever more sit at any table they might choose.

Towards the evening the spider woke up at last, and looked for the fire, but it was gone. Quickly he spun himself a piece of web, and holding this above his head, was wafted by the breeze to the royal castle. He listened to what was going on there, and heard everybody cheering the fly for having brought beneficial fire out of the chasm of Hell.

The spider was furious, and elbowed his way among the courtiers straight before the king, who was at dinner, smiling contentedly. There were candles burning on his table and a fire crackling in the fireplace. On the table the fly was strutting in her glittering new dress coat, and nibbling at a fried haunch of a boar.

"Your Majesty, it was me who fetched the fire from the abyss of Hell," cried the spider bitterly. "And this thief of a fly stole it from me!"

"Do not believe him, Your Majesty. Chase him away, the arrant liar!" buzzed the fly angrily. "For you saw with your own eyes that it was me who brought the fire, and not the wily spider!"

However, the king, being a just man, subjected the spider to strict questioning and wanted to know how he had got down into the pit of Hell.

"I spun myself a mighty long rope and used it to descend into Hell's ravine. It must still be hanging there," the spider bravely defended himself.

The king sent servants to the edge of the abyss to fetch the spider's rope. But they did not find it there. It must have slipped off the boulder, fallen down and burnt. When the servants came back without the rope, the king came to believe the fly and drove the poor spider away.

Since those times the spider has hated flies, and revenged himself for the robbery on the entire troublesome and cheeky progeny. He spreads his transparent webs in every corner and whichever fly gets caught in them is mercilessly destroyed.

Flies, on the other hand, have asserted their right to sit with men at every table: indeed, they have a scroll with three royal seals certifying this right!

The Blue Kerchief

Linda was no beauty, rather the opposite. She was a thin little girl, all arms and legs. She had pale cheeks covered with freckles and hair wispy as a mouse's tail.

Linda was an orphan. She went barefoot nearly all the year round; only when snow fell, she scrounged worn-out old shoes from somewhere, and threw a patched-up woollen scarf over her flimsy little dress.

She went about the village from one cottage to another, from one house to another. And everywhere there was some work for her to do.

One day at harvest time she minded some children, and got a small jug of milk and a slice of bread in reward for her pains. Another time she tended geese by the brook all day for a plate of cabbage soup and a potato pancake. At the farm before the weekend she usually earned a piece of bacon, sometimes even some lunch for scrubbing the floor in the big room.

At night she went to a rich widow who let her sleep overnight on the straw in the barn. In winter-time she allowed her to stay with the cows, for it was warm in the cowshed. Of course, not even the night's bed was really free. The mean farmer's widow made the girl do quite a bit of work for her.

After the harvest, when the granary was full of corn, the farmer's wife kept

Linda working full time. She brought an ancient handmill from the loft, and from morning till night Linda had to grind the corn with it. She would grind on and on until her arms were stiff with exhaustion and her legs gave way under her from standing up all day.

Every evening the widow came to inspect the work done. When Linda had ground a sackful of flour, she was content, and would bring her a plate of spuds with cabbage. But when the sack was not full the woman reviled her for being a lazy-bones, and then the girl would go to bed without supper.

One day, an old beggar came to the farm asking for alms. The miserly widow banged the door in his face.

As the disappointed old man was creeping along to the gate, he suddenly heard a sad song coming out of the barn.

Carefully he opened the door a crack, and saw a thin girl standing in front of a sack grinding corn on an old-fashioned handmill, and singing softly.

"Good morning, dear maiden," the old man greeted her gently. "May I sit down here with you for a while? I am pretty tired from walking all the day."

Linda was a little frightened, but when she looked into the old man's forget-me-not blue eyes, all fear left her. This is a way only a good, just man can look, she said to herself, and bade him sit down on a sack by the wall.

The old man settled down comfortably and started asking questions:

"Is it your task to grind a whole sack of corn on this little grinder? I feel sorry for you."

"It is not exactly hard work," said Linda with a sigh, "but believe me, sometimes in the evening I can hardly stretch my stiff arms, and my legs feel like lead."

"I believe you, little maiden," the beggar said. Then he fished in his bag, pulled out a pouch of corn and said, "They have given me a handful of corn in the neighbouring cottage. Would you mind grinding it for me, when you have done with yours?"

"With pleasure. Just give it to me, and I will grind it at once," said the maiden and poured the old man's corn into the handmill. She turned the handle a few times, and there was a handful of flour in the old man's pouch.

"Thank you kindly," said the old man delightedly. "Now please bake a pancake out of that flour of mine. I haven't eaten for two days."

Linda willingly kneaded the flour into dough, and made a good crisp pancake for the poor hungry man. The old man enjoyed the pancake tremendously, and then, having picked up carefully every little crumb, made a new request.

"Kind little maiden, could you fetch me a drop of fresh water? The pancake was really excellent, but I need to wash it down a bit."

Linda hurried to the well in the courtyard, and brought some fresh water from the fountain for the old man to drink. He drank with relish, wiped his chin, and said, "You are a really good girl, Linda. Your hands are stiff from work, and yet you ground the corn and baked a pancake for me. You have been on your legs all day, and yet you fetch fresh water for me from the well. I am a poor man, my dear, but you have been so obliging I will give you a souvenir to remember me by."

The old man put his hand into his bag made of strings, pulled out a blue kerchief, and handed it to her, saying, "This little kerchief is sure to bring you some comfort and joy. When you go to bed, tie it round your head, and before you drop off to sleep, think of something nice and good. Then you will dream about it, and sometimes your dream may even come true."

Linda was dumbfounded with joy. Never in her life had she seen such a fine kerchief, and now it was hers. When she recovered she wanted to thank the old man, but he had vanished; only the wicket gate was heard to creak a little.

In the evening when her work was done, Linda got ready for bed. She tied the blue kerchief round her head, shut her eyes, recalled the old man's words, and wanted to think of something nice. But she just could not do it.

In a short while tiredness made her fall fast asleep, and the last thing she thought of was the confounded grinder whose handle she would have to turn like a drudge the next day. If she only could get rid of that thing, she would feel happy.

Suddenly and quite gently Linda crossed the threshold of everyday existence, and found herself in the delightful bluish world of dreams. She dreamt she was racing on a black horse across a snowy plain. Snow was glittering everywhere, and soft snowflakes were gently striking her face.

"Where are you taking me, my dear little horse?" asked Linda smiling happily and holding on fast to the silver mane of the racing black steed.

A small turret appeared on a knoll in the distance, and that was where her horse was heading. When they got nearer, the girl saw it was neither a castle nor a church, but an ordinary windmill. However, there was something strange about the place. Though the rattling and creaking of the millstones could be heard from inside the mill, the wings were hanging down limp without moving an inch even when the wind was blowing.

The black horse stopped outside the mill. Linda jumped off him quickly, and ran through the open door straight into the grinding room.

She stared and stared in sheer amazement, and what was it she saw? A large decorated chest in the middle of the mill and from there the rattling sound was coming. A sack of corn was on the box, and the grain was falling down in a thin stream into the funnel on the lid. And below, coming out of a hole in the side, flour was mounting like a snowdrift. And not a living soul anywhere. In vain did Linda look all round, in vain did she call into every corner. There was no one to be seen.

"Oh dear, what pleasure it would be to take this wondrous thing home to the barn with me!" thought the little girl, but the oak chest was extremely heavy. She could not move it; she was not even able to lift the top and have a look inside.

"How could I possibly get this magic chest home?" Linda thought hard, but there was nothing she could figure out. At that moment, the black horse outside neighed and impatiently kicked the earth with his hoof in the doorway. That was enough for the maiden. At once she hit upon a happy idea.

She looked round the grinding room and saw a length of strong rope hanging behind the beam, probably a sailor's cable. She tied one end round the chest, the other she put the horse to. Then she urged him on, the horse pulled hard, the rope went taut and the chest moved. In a moment it was out on the snow. Linda sat down on it, and flew with the wind at her back as though in a sledge. She held fast to the funnel, with her blue kerchief flying, and the black horse raced across the snow-covered plain till showers of glittering snow flew off his hoofs.

Before she knew it, they had stopped outside the widow's barn. The gate stood wide open, so they drove straight inside. However, as they were riding over the threshold, the chest jolted, sprang up, and Linda's kerchief slid off her head on to her shoulders. At that moment her magic dream was over.

In the morning Linda woke up smiling.

"Oh, a thousand pities that it was all but a dream," she sighed aloud, gently stroking her blue kerchief. But when she entered the barn, she stood dumbfounded with amazement.

In the middle of the barn on the threshing floor stood the painted chest, the very chest she had longed for in her dream. She fed a handful of corn into the funnel, and all at once, there was clattering and rattling inside, and pure white flour poured out of the lower hole.

Thus, from now on Linda's work became much lighter. She added the corn in handfuls, and flour poured into the sack fastened below. By the evening she now had three, or sometimes even four sacks full of flour, and what is more, she was not at all tired. She sang happily as she worked. And that is how it went from day to day.

At first the miserly woman was astonished. She did not think it right that this weak girl should, all of a sudden, grind so much flour in a day. She even thought that the girl was assisted by some dark powers, a witch, or a household imp. But then she let the idea of magic go, and was content to get used to the row of white sacks.

One day, however, the widow crossed the yard, and peeped through a chink between the open door into the barn. She saw Linda sitting on a large painted chest, feeding handfuls of grain into the opening in the top, and singing merrily at her work.

"Well," said the widow to herself. "I had suspected long ago that the wench was not grinding the corn on my handmill and using the handle. Who could have got this magic chest for her? No matter who it was — most likely it was Beelzebub himself — but that's no matter. The main thing is that the chest stands in my barn and grinds as much flour as I am likely to need. And it would grind even more if the lazy-bones did not pour in the grain by small handfuls." So she made up her mind she would work the chest herself.

"But first I must get rid of the wench," she decided, "and then I shall grind flour for the whole village. Goodness, I shall have bags of money! I may become the richest farmer's wife in the land."

Avarice has already brought ruin on many people, but probably that is what the widow did not know.

The very next day at the break of dawn she woke Linda and told her they would go to the forest to fetch wood. The farmer's wife put on her fur-coat, Linda wrapped herself in her woollen scarf, and they set out. The widow sat on the box, and drove the waggon herself. For a long time they were driving through the forest until they got to a dense underwood which the sun never penetrated, and where not a single bird was singing.

Here the widow made Linda get off, telling her to gather some wood, while she herself would look for some cranberries.

So Linda set about gathering and piling up dry branches. She had long been ready, but the woman did not come. For a long time she waited for her, looking, calling out, but all in vain.

Meanwhile, the widow was driving fast back home with her head full of thoughts of the painted chest. So she had got rid of that freckled wench, who would never come back from the forest. She was sure to get torn to pieces by wolves, or strangled by a bear. And now the chest would be hers and hers alone!

No sooner did she get home than she went to the barn, and threw a few handfuls of grain into the funnel. There was rattling inside the chest, and flour poured out down below.

"I will not get rich quickly if I do it in such small handfuls," decided the miserly farmer's wife, and seizing a whole sackful of grain, she poured it into the funnel all at once.

Inside it rattled and cracked, and then everything fell silent — the grinding was over.

The widow took fright, and tried to open the top of the chest to see what had gone wrong. But the lid stuck fast as if hammered down with nails, and she could not move it an inch. All her nails got broken as she clambered to get inside, but the lid would not budge. Then she saw an iron crowbar in the corner. She grabbed it, set it into the chink near the funnel and, using all her strength, got the lid loose at last. In her curiosity she bent over the edge of the chest. All of a sudden, flames burst out from it, and gripping her like a pair of fiery hands, dragged her inside. Then the lid dropped noisily, the millstone gave a rattling sound, and it was not flour but a little pile of ashes that came out of the bottom hole. And that was the end of the miserly farmer's wife.

Meanwhile, Linda was still in the forest waiting for her. When it began to grow dark and she saw all her waiting was in vain, she set out on her journey back home. However, the forest was getting thicker and thicker, so she missed the path, and lost her way. When darkness fell, everything seemed to spring to life. The trees were turning into giant figures, and as the wind blew, they were groping for Linda with their leafy arms. Owls were flitting silently among them like ghostly shadows and hooting woefully. Over the marsh in the ferns tiny lights of fire-flies were swarming and the swarming was accompanied by a horrible choir of croaking frogs. Somewhere, not far off, a stag bellowed.

Linda was no coward, and she decided she would stay in the wood overnight. She would be sure to find her way more easily in the morning.

She climbed on to a spreading oak-tree so that no beast might get at her. Having settled comfortably in the branches, she tied her blue kerchief firmly

round her head, so that she might have another lovely dream. And what were her thoughts and wishes before she fell asleep?

Well, first she wanted to get out of the thick woods. Then she would like to grind flour again in that painted chest, not only for the miserly widow but for all her neighbours, and merely for a good word so that they might get fond of her. In addition, she would like to be prettier and have new clothes so that she might go to the inn for a dance with the other girls.

She dreamed of all the things she had thought of when falling asleep. She was led out of the forest by a big coloured bird. At home there was the painted chest waiting for her in the barn. The miserly farmer's wife was nowhere to be seen. Linda looked after the farm on her own with great success. In the lumber-room, a lovely new dress was hanging ready for her to wear. When she put it on and looked into the mirror, she could not believe her eyes: what she saw was a pretty girl with curly hair, and at the dance none of the lads could take his eyes off her.

It was a lovely dream and Linda was smiling happily all night. Probably she had a feeling all this might come true again. And so it did.

In the morning she was awakened by the shrill voice of a jay sitting on a branch opposite her. Linda realized that it was the big bird with coloured feathers of her dream who was calling her. So she followed the jay's voice until she got out of the wood. After this she easily found her way to the village.

The widow had really vanished from the farm, and as she had no relatives, Linda now stayed there alone, looking after everything, particularly the painted chest, so that it might not remain idle. She ground all her neighbours' corn for the winter, and people loved her for her readiness to help.

"What a fine lass Linda has become! Now all she needs is to marry," they would say. And this also happened. So now Linda and her husband grind flour for the whole village and even the neighbouring district. Theirs is a good life, they are happy and contented.

A Greater Coward
than the Hare

The hare was sitting in his little den in a self-pitying mood saying, "What a sorrowful life I am leading! I can hardly stick out my nose from here without someone trying to do away with me. The wolf, the fox, the lynx ... and how many hunters wander about the forest with their hounds!"

Then he looked furtively at the sky and mused, "And what about the birds of prey? The eagle and the hawk haunt me by day, the owl by night. Oh, what misery I am in: such a life is not worth living!"

The hare complained about his fate and the world until he came to the conclusion that he was indeed the most miserable creature alive, that there was no one who had to live in constant fear the way he had to, and that he had better go and drown himself in the lake. So he went, all in tears, and could hardly see where he was going, until he got to the edge of the water. And there, suddenly, he heard plump, plump, plump! All around him the frogs began to jump into the water, terrified there was someone tramping in the sedge who was waiting to swallow them.

For a while, the hare watched the frogs like one transported, but then he started laughing till he nearly split his sides:

"Just look, even I am feared. Even I, the timid hare, inspire fear in others, ha, ha, ha!"

And the hare laughed until his upper lip burst (and he has had it split in two halves ever since). Then he stopped, but that did not lower his spirits in any way.

Once again he was happy to be alive, and gave up every thought of drowning himself. But he did not feel like returning to the woods. So he decided to go out into the wide world and find himself good friends and a suitable dwelling-place.

Knowing it would be a long way to go, and he would need to take provisions, he made himself a small two-wheeled cart out of reeds and willow-twigs, yoked himself to the beam and set out at a fresh pace.

He went along singing, setting the rhythm with his ears, and before long he met an old cobbler's thread.

"Where are you going?" asked the hare.

"I don't know where, and I don't know which way," replied the thread. "What's more, I am old now, and find walking difficult."

"Well, sit down in my little cart," said the hare, and now they were two.

They were now singing in two voices, and though the thread's voice was rather sharp, found it better going all the same.

Then they saw a pin and a needle.

"Where are you off to?" called the hare from the distance.

And the pin said, "Into the wide world. Only we don't know where and which way, we find it hard going in the high grass . . ."

"Well, come and sit in my cart," the hare invited them, and having helped them up into the cart, yoked himself again to the shaft with a good heart.

However, he had not had time to get going properly, and the pilgrims had not even set their voices for another song, before they saw a red-hot ember. He was sizzling and smoking in the grass till the hare shouted angrily:

"Hello, you over there! Roll to the side a little so that I don't run you over. And what exactly are you doing here?"

"I have set out into the world, and can go no further," moaned the ember. "Please, hare, take me into your cart, you will not be sorry."

Well, a red-hot ember is always good for making fire, mused the hare. But how to go about it so that he should not burn through the cart?

In the end, however, it proved quite simple. The hare put a flat stone on the bottom of the cart, the ember sat down on it, and so all five of them set out on their further travels.

For a long time they did not meet a living soul until they reached the spot where the road turned towards a little pond, where they saw a duck.

And, without much ado, the duck started questioning the hare:

"Out on a picnic, out on a picnic? And who is it you are taking in that pretty little cart of yours?"

"It's no picnic we are out for," replied the hare with dignity. "The thread, the pin, the needle, the ember and I are going into the wide world. Come and join us if you like ..."

"Only too glad, only too glad," agreed the duck without even letting the hare finish what he had to say. She fell into step with him, took the shaft under her wing, and so they were six.

They journeyed over hill and dale, across fields and meadows, till darkness began to fall. At once the hare and the duck started looking for a place to spend the night, and were overjoyed to see a little cottage standing by the road. It was among the bushes and so cunningly hidden that it would have been hard to discover, yet the hare did notice it and made straight for the door with his cart.

He opened it boldly, and when they found there was not a soul inside, each of the little pilgrims laid himself to sleep as his fancy took him.

The duck in the tub full of pure water which stood behind the door, the pin fell asleep stuck in a towel, the ember on the stone table which made it nice and cool for his back. The thread and the needle lay down in the bed, and the hare crept into the sweet-smelling hay in the little loft.

Tired as they were after the day's travelling, they were all fast asleep before you could count up to five. Then the only sound heard in the little cottage was the sleepers' calm breathing. Above, the silvery moon started his slow journey across the sky.

At midnight, however, some heavy steps were heard on the road. It was the owner of the cottage — a fearful robber — coming home. Tired out, he threw on the floor the sack with golden coins he had taken from people during the day, opened the door, and automatically leaned over the tub to allay his thirst after the day's work.

But the robber was in for a surprise! The sleepy duck struck the water with both her wings so that it splashed and for a moment blinded him. And then things started happening in quick succession. He tried to dry himself and the pin stuck him in the face. So he ran to the table, where he was burnt by the glowing ember. In the end, when he was entirely bewildered, he jumped into the bed and landed with his back on the pointed needle and thread!

In that thick darkness the robber thought there was a whole regiment of soldiers lying in wait for him in the cottage with drawn sabres and rifles. And when the hare started thumping in the loft, the man ran through the open door and pelted off, as if a whole army were at his heels.

He never returned to the cottage. And so the hare and his friends were able not only to sleep quietly till the morning, but to stay and live there until their last days. The gold coins left behind by the robber outside the cottage made their life even pleasanter.

The King's Counsellor

Once upon a time there lived a king, and believe it or not he was a just man.

He did not oppress his subjects. On the contrary, he was anxious to know how they lived and worked, and how they fared in his kingdom.

To see this with his own eyes, he changed now and then into simple clothes and went unrecognized among the people.

One day he came to a village in his disguise, and there he saw a man digging a ditch by the road.

"What are you doing?" asked the king.

"Can't you see? My master has ordered me to dig a ditch," replied the man sullenly, and went on throwing the earth up from the bottom.

"It's hard work you've got," said the king.

"I should say so," fumed the digger wiping the sweat off his forehead. "From dawn to dusk I've got to swing this spade, just to earn a piece of bread."

"You must earn a lot of money for all that toil, don't you?" the king asked.

"Well, there might be enough, but what is left when I have divided the wages is just enough for garlic soup," answered the digger and went on delving into the earth.

"Then you must be dividing it wrongly," rejoined the king.

"What's wrong about it? Look," explained the digger, straightening his back and leaning on the spade. "One part of my earnings is thrown into the water, the second goes to pay my debt, the third, and that's the largest one, I lend, and the fourth, that's the smallest part, that is hardly enough to keep me and my wife from starving."

The king, all puzzled, shook his head, waved to the man and went his way. He kept pondering the man's words, but could not find any reasonable explanation for them.

Towards evening when he was coming back to the city, he saw the digger still working in the ditch.

The king stopped near him, and addressed him in a friendly way:

"Listen, man, I am your king. Sometimes I go abroad in disguise to see with my own eyes how my people live and what they talk about. I have been thinking about the odd way you divide your wages, and just cannot get to the bottom of it. Explain it to me, and I will pay you three gold ducats. Here you are."

The digger put away his spade, thanked the king for the ducats, wrapped them carefully in a scarf, and hid them under his cap. Then he started to explain: "You see, Your Majesty, it's like this: With the first part of the wages I buy salt, and then I throw it into the water from which I make my soup. We can't do without salt, you know, and at present it is terribly expensive, your ministers have put a heavy tax on it. The second part, that is the debt I pay off to my parents for having brought me up and fed me. If I didn't take care of them now and give them money to live on, they would have to go begging in their old age. The third part, the largest, that's the money I spend on my children. That is the loan, as I hope that one day when I am old, they are going to pay it back. Well, and the remainder of the wage, that is just about enough to feed my wife and myself, to preserve our strength to go on working. So now you know, Your Majesty, how your people live!"

The king thought a while, and said, "Your words are good and instructive. You have given me a fine explanation of what they mean, but do not give this away to anyone until you see me again. Understand?"

The digger understood. He bowed to the king, and briskly went on working. He had to catch up with the time he had lost by talking, and the dusk was nearly about to fall.

The very next day the king summoned all the noblemen to his presence and put the digger's riddle to them.

"The person who solves this," he said, "will become my first counsellor."

The barons, earls and princes all pondered, thought hard, racked their brains, but none af them hit upon anything.

"What blockheads you all are!" the king derided them and drove them out of his castle.

Afterwards he summoned the lower gentry, the squires and yeomen — these are supposed to be rather more clever.

But none of them could explain the digger's riddle either.

However, among them was the squire for whom the digger was working. On his way back from the castle, he found the man by the road still busily engaged in digging the ditch. He stopped to have a chat with him.

"I went to see the king," boasted the master. "His Majesty gave us such a strange riddle. How will you explain, he said, that someone throws one part of his poor wages into water, one part goes to pay off his debt, and a further part, the largest one, he uses as a loan?"

"And could anyone explain that?" the digger asked with curiosity.

"How could they! No one was able to solve that mystery." And the squire waved his hand.

"You won't believe me, sir, but I know the correct answer," laughed the digger.

"You don't say so! You are pulling my leg, aren't you?"

"Not at all. It was me who thought up the riddle, and so I must know the answer," said the digger and told the farmer how he had met the disguised king.

The farmer urged the digger to give him the answer, adding that he would give him three gold coins for it.

"That's not enough," said the sly digger. "The king gave me three ducats. You must give me twice as much."

The squire fidgeted a little, but then he gave the digger twice three ducats, learnt the correct answer, and rushed back to the castle to tell the king to appoint him his first counsellor.

The king was astonished, but then he realized that the digger must be working on the squire's estate, and so he took the man heavily to task:

"You got the answer from your digger, didn't you? Do not try to deny it."

The squire tried to back out, but it is not right to tell lies to a king. So in the end he came out with the truth.

The king was furious, sent the squire away, and at once sent his bailiff to fetch the digger.

"You have not kept our agreement, you rogue! I will have you thrown into the deepest dungeon," the king shouted at the poor digger when the latter was brought before him.

But the digger defended himself boldly:

"I did not break our agreement, Your Majesty. You said I must not give away the answer to anyone until I see you again. And I have seen you as many as nine times today!"

"What stuff and nonsense is that? Where did you see me nine times?" said the amazed king, rising from his throne.

"Here," said the digger softly, and stretched out his hand before the king. He had all the nine ducats on his palm, each with the king's head coined upon it.

The king stared at his likeness engraved on the gold coins. Then he understood, and burst out laughing. "You are a good fellow, digger. You with your clever head far surpass all my noblemen. You are going to be my counsellor!"

Ever since the king of that country took the simple man for his counsellor, everyone has had enough bread, and led a good and happy life.

The Maiden
from the Oak Frame

There was once a young fisherman living with his mother on the seashore. The old woman was always mending torn nets, and the son used them to catch silvery fish. Sometimes he caught a lot, at other times just a few, depending on the generosity of the sea. And so the two led a happy and contented life.

After a time, however, a bad illness afflicted his mother. She was withering away, drying up, until it looked as if she would go out at a breath. She never even left the hut lest the wind from the bay should blow her down into the sea. One day she lay down, crossed her arms on her bosom, fell asleep, and never woke up again.

The young fisherman cried bitterly, for he had no one in the whole world now. He did not feel any joy in returning from his fishing expeditions to the cold, comfortless room. So he often sailed far, far out to sea.

One day he had no fisherman's luck from the very morning, as though out of spite all fish avoided his net. Towards midday, when his native shore had disappeared behind him, the sky became overcast with dark clouds which hid the sun like a black wall. Grey twilight descended upon the sea's surface, and the wind, weak at first, grew stronger and drove the fisherman's bark far out on to the open sea. The young man rolled up the sail so as not to have it torn down by the gale, pulled up the empty net, and grabbed the rudder. He tried to turn the boat towards home, but in vain.

Only towards evening did the wind drop and the waves subside. Quite near on his port side the fisherman suddenly saw black rocks and a large sailing ship with broken masts. It had got stuck on a rocky cliff and been abandoned by the crew. Who knows what tempest had blown it into those parts?

He climbed aboard. The ship was empty and deserted. Not even a mouse or a rat crossed his path as he roamed the devastated holds of the wreck. Down at the very bottom he found the captain's cabin. He had to force open the door under which seaweed had been caught in a layer of mud. Inside, nothing but musty void breathed upon him. A large painting in a heavy oak frame hung over a narrow bed — a portrait of a lovely maiden. She had a flood of golden hair and violet eyes. Wherever the fisherman stood in the cabin, her look never left him. As soon as he had recovered from his astonishment, he took the picture down from the wall with great care and said softly to himself, "No, no, I won't leave you here all alone like this. I will take you home with me; at least I shan't feel so lonely." And that was what he did.

That very night, he hung the picture up in his cottage on the front wall opposite the door.

"At least you will bid me welcome whenever I enter the room," he said casually to the maiden in the oak frame.

Before he fell asleep, excited and tired out after the long day, he looked at the gentle face and had a feeling that her thoughtful eyes rested on him with a searching look.

"You must be the daughter of the captain who was wrecked on the rocky cliffs and he must have perished. Otherwise he would not have left you all alone in that abandoned wreck. I have fallen in love with you at first sight, my beauty, and rejoice to think that now I shall have you with me all the time." After bidding the maiden goodnight he put out the lamp.

From the day he hung the mysterious picture on the wall, it was as if the fisherman's whole life was transformed. He was happy to come home from his fishing. No sooner did he step over the threshold than the kind violet eyes gave him their welcome, and, afterwards kept him company, following him all the evening. Before going to sleep, the fisherman would sit down opposite the picture, contemplating the kind sweet face, and sometimes he would tell her softly about his mother, his fishing on the sea, the merchant who bought his fish and cheated him, the magnificent conches and brownish-gold nuggets of amber which the tide cast up on the sandy beach, and about the marvellous flowers in the rocky ravines which were the same colour as her eyes.

Thus the days passed, and the cottage seemed to have found its peace and good cheer again.

One evening the fisherman returned from the sea tired and hungry. He ate his supper quickly, because there was the old net to mend for the morrow. Then he spread it out across the room, but in vain did he look for holes: the net was mended so well it was as good as new. Greatly puzzled, he wondered how this was possible. It may still have been the work of his late mother, he thought. When he gazed at the picture again before going to sleep, he had a feeling that the violet eyes gave him a faint, tender smile.

"This must be only a dream," he said to himself drowsily, and fell asleep.

When he returned home from his fishing the next day, he was in for a new surprise: the room was tidied up, the window open and washed clean.

"I must have forgotten to shut it, and the rain has washed it," said the fisherman to explain the mystery to himself, and placed a bunch of white honeysuckles, which he had plucked on his way from the harbour, on the shelf under the picture.

Before he went to sleep he told the golden-haired maiden about his mother, how she kept the little room spick and span and cosy, and that he took after her in this respect, being very orderly himself. And again he had a feeling that the violet eyes rested on him with an intimate look, and the maiden gave him a gentle touch of a smile.

On the third day, when the fisherman returned late in the evening from the sea which had been tempestuous, and for hours would not let his bark enter the harbour, he understood at a glance that all that was going on in the cottage was not happening of itself.

The maiden's face in the picture had an impatient, even anxious look on it, but the violet eyes were tender and smiling. A fire was crackling in the fireplace, the table was laid, and on it was a plate of steaming soup and freshly baked bread.

The fisherman was baffled. He looked at the fair face in the picture, but the golden-haired maiden only smiled, her silent mouth being unable to explain anything to him. He gave some fresh water to the flowers under the picture, and went to bed, but could not fall asleep for a long time. He tossed from side to side on his bed, and it was nearly dawn before he finally contrived how he would get to the bottom of the mystery.

No sooner had the sun risen above the horizon than he picked up his nets, his fishing tackle and his oars, and directed his steps straight to the harbour. There he put his fishing outfit into the boat, and, taking a detour, silently set out for home again. Already at a distance he could hear a voice calling the fowls for feeding. He tiptoed to the window, looked inside, and just could not believe his eyes: the oak frame on the wall was empty and the picture of the golden-haired maiden was gone. Silently he stole to the fence, and looking into the little backyard stood petrified with amazement. The maiden from the picture stood on the porch, a basket in hand, pouring grain to the hens and driving away the cock with a smile on her face.

That day the fisherman did not sail out fishing. His soul was in turmoil; he did not know what to do in order not to break the spell.

At last he decided to go and seek advice from a good old fortune-teller, who lived on the end of the bay in a hut made of clay, with a black tomcat and a wise owl. That old woman knew a remedy for every human pain and woe.

"She has helped so many people, perhaps she will help me, too," said the fisherman to himself as he knocked at the bulging door made of larch-tree bark.

"I know your worry," the hag welcomed him. "It's the captain's daughter from the picture, isn't it? You are in love with her, and would be happier to have her about in the room alive than just painted in an oak frame." And it was simple advice she gave him: When the fair maiden leaves the picture, let him quickly take the frame down, hide it in the store-room, and lock it with three turns of the key.

"Hang the key on your neck and never take it off! When the maiden doesn't find the frame, she won't be able to return into the picture, and will be glad to stay with you."

The fisherman bowed low to the wise old woman, thanked her, and promised to bring her the whole of his next catch.

Then he did everything exactly as she had advised him.

The next morning he again returned home unobserved. He waited behind the wall until he heard the girl's voice in the courtyard, then he crawled into the room through the window, took down the empty frame, hid it in the store-room, which he locked with three turns of the key, and hung the key on a piece of hemp cord round his neck. Everything went well, just as the wise fortune-teller had predicted.

When the violet-eyed maiden saw the empty wall, she took fright and looked for the oak frame. Unable to find it, she started crying. But she quietened down

after a while, and in the evening she sat down at the laid table together with the fisherman for the first time.

The young fisherman was a good man, and so they lived happily together in their cottage on the seashore. After a time a baby son was born to them. Handsome, in looks like his mother, he inherited from his father his strength and his love of the sea. He grew apace and was his parents' great joy. When he came of age, he was enticed by the distant shores, and sailed away into the wide world as a cabin-boy on a large ship. His mother found it hard to say goodbye to her son, but his father wished for his son to voyage as he had never been able to himself. "Just sail on, my son, into the wide world; there you'll get to know many lands and many men. You are strong, hard-working and reasonable, maybe one day you'll come back as a captain."

Many years passed. The fisherman had become a white-haired old man, his strength was leaving him, he no longer dared to go out to the sea himself. The gold hair of his wife was now sprinkled with silvery snow, but she was still beautiful, and her violet eyes were as young and sparkling as they had been years before when she stepped out of the picture.

What the old fisherman liked best in those days was sitting on the porch watching the sea, and patiently waiting, day after day, for a sailing ship with three masts to appear, with his son as captain. Several times a year the son would come to see his parents, bringing them exotic presents, and after spending a happy time with them, he would sail off to faraway countries again.

And so one day in autumn the old fisherman's time came to depart from his life. His good heart came to a standstill. When his wife was putting on his burial clothes she saw the key round his neck. At once she guessed it would be the key to the store-room which had been locked all those long years. Taking the key, she unlocked the store-room, and there, among the fishing nets, she found the heavy oak frame. She gave it a smile as if to welcome a good old friend, dusted and polished it, and hung it on the front wall where it had hung so long ago. And having lit a wax candle at her husband's head, she silently re-entered the frame.

It may have been a coincidence that the son — now a captain — returned from a distant voyage that very evening. He found his native cottage locked and deserted. In the room lay his dead father with the candle dying away, but his mother had vanished.

Still he looked round — and what did he see? His mother was smiling at him from the picture on the wall. She was young and beautiful the way he remembered her from his early childhood.

Tears rushed to his eyes. "I had no idea," he said to himself, "that father had mother's picture painted. How much he must have loved her."

The next day he buried the old fisherman, locked the little cottage with nine turns of the key, and took his mother's picture along with the frame to his ship. He hung it in his cabin over his bed, and every evening before he slept he looked into her eyes, and talked to her softly, just as his father had done years before.

Cough and Ague

One autumn, the weather was so miserable that it was not fit for a dog to endure. For days on end it rained, pastures and forests were soaked with water, and people stayed inside their houses.

Only young Jurgis took his rifle every morning, and set out for the woods. He was such a passionate hunter that he did not in the least mind the foul weather, even though all the game sought shelter from the rain, and he usually came back empty-handed.

"At least I get some fresh air," he would say to his parents and his wife with a smile, while they, seeing him so wet and bedraggled, only shook their heads and wondered if such hunting was at all worth the trouble.

One night it was raining more heavily than ever, but Jurgis kept waking up, lest he should miss his hunt for the bear.

The next day, he found the bear's lair under the old oak empty, and there was no trace of the bear. So the hunter crouched in the brushwood, shivering with cold while rain ran down the back of his neck.

Some hours passed, and eventually Jurgis heard some peculiar growling, whining and croaking, as if someone were talking; yet it did not sound at all like human speech.

Jurgis peeped out cautiously from his hiding-place, and under the oak he saw an ugly old man and woman. The very sight of them sent shivers down his spine.

The old man's face was yellow, his nose reached down to his waist, his claw-like fingers would have done more honour to a crow, and when he spoke, he shook all over with coughing, sputtering and sneezing.

"This is the kind of weather that I, Cough, enjoy best. When the weather is dry and warm, I do not appear a great deal in the world, and frost doesn't do me any good either. But today I will easily get quite close to people, and am already looking forward to the way I am going to harass them."

"You are right, godfather," agreed the old woman. "People also find it hard to protect themselves from me, Ague, in this foul weather, and that's why I am off to that cottage over there."

"Oh, what rogues you are!" thought Jurgis, gazing at the old crony. And indeed, she was a sight, shaking all over until her enormous fishy eyes nearly dropped out of her green face. Like the old man, she was arrayed in threadbare rags dripping with dirt.

"How will you go about it?" asked Cough.

The hag just laughed.

"It's quite simple, you yourself know the way. People here like the sauna even in rainy weather. They make their bodies hot with steam, flog themselves with little whips, and after that they drink cold water straight from the jug. Well, I will hide in that jug so that they drink me up with the water. Then I can torment them to my heart's content. Ague is not at all easy to drive out of the body."

"You're right, I'll do the same thing," said the old man. "So let's go together. I've grown feeble with the long waiting."

When they rose and set out for the cottage, Jurgis did not tarry either, for he would not let Cough and Ague nestle down in his home.

He ran for all he was worth, and arrived just in time. His father had returned from the sauna, and was on the point of pouring himself cold water from the jug.

"Don't drink that!" cried Jurgis, taking the jug from the old man's hand. Whereupon he poured all the water into a leather bag, and having tied up the neck of the bag thoroughly, hung it up in the chimney so that in the pungent smoke Cough and Ague should get what they both deserved.

Since that day the whole family and the neighbours have often come and looked into the chimney to see how Ague is shaking the bag, and to listen to the coughing that can be heard from inside every now and then. Jurgis may have shown that wonderful bag even to you.

Be that as it may, the people in that part of the country always refrain from drinking cold water, no matter how hot they might be.

The Three Brothers

Far up in the north there was once a Kingdom of Snow ruled by a wise old king. He lived in a crystal palace with a thousand windows, and behind each a bright star glimmered with cold bluish light.

The king had three sons. The eldest, Wind, was wise and prudent like his father. Gale, the younger one, was rash, a true dare-devil; the youngest, Blizzard, had not a bit of good nature in him, he was a malicious bully and whatever he took into his head to do, he did.

The king was getting weary of his ruler's duties, having held the reign for over three hundred years, so he decided to hand over the crystal palace and the snowy realm to one of his sons. But to which of them should it go?

"I must put them to a test. Whichever is the best husbandman will also make a good ruler," he decided and summoned his sons.

Giving each of them three ducats he said, "He who makes the best use of the money within a short time will receive the palace and the whole kingdom."

First to set out impatiently into the world was Blizzard, his youngest son.

Wherever he flew, he left behind him a frosty trace and broken drift-ice. He flew through villages blocking lakes, rivers and brooks with ice. Then he flew through the towns and made all wells freeze over.

Outside one of the towns he caught up with a sledge. It was driven by a rich merchant muffled up to his ears in his fox fur coat.

Blizzard attacked him with all his might, and roared at him, "Give me three ducats, or I will make you freeze to the bone!"

But the merchant did not hear him. His fur cap was pulled down over his ears, and he had folded his fur collar over it.

Blizzard grew angry, and having got under the merchant's fur coat he penetrated through the caftan under the shirt, and the poor man froze to the bone and tumbled into the sledge half dead.

"Well, you icicle, there is no ducat to be wangled out of you," said Blizzard with an evil laugh, and flew on.

On the edge of the forest he spotted a woodcutter, who was digging out stumps.

"This one is good for at least one ducat," thought Blizzard, and pounced upon the poor peasant.

But the woodcutter at his work was swinging his axe so mightily that the sweat was pouring off him. Blizzard did not know from which side to attack the fellow. As if to spite him, the man threw aside his short fur coat, took off his gloves, and hewed away at the stumps in his shirt sleeves.

"But I will get at you," Blizzard whistled furiously, and slipped into the gloves the woodcutter had laid aside.

"When you put these on, your hands will freeze into an icicle!" And in no time the gloves turned into lumps of ice, becoming hard as stone.

Having uprooted the last stump, the woodcutter made ready to go home. He put on his sheepskin and his fur cap, and was about to slip on his gloves, but they were hard as horn.

"Oh dear," he said, "they are hard as a bone, and would not warm my hands, I must squeeze them a bit."

He placed the gloves on a little stump, and using the handle of the axe dealt them such powerful blows that he nearly killed Blizzard, who was hiding inside. The latter fled so quickly that on his way he dropped even those three ducats he had got from his royal father.

After such a thrashing Blizzard did not feel like travelling any longer and returned home in very low spirits.

"Well, well, my son," the king welcomed his youngest. "The money I gave you is gone, and to boot, you are bruised all over. At least you know now that a man who works hard has a strong hand. And remember: You should help people, not hurt them!"

The elder brothers nodded their heads in agreement without a twinge of pity for the youngest.

"Now I will show you how people are to be helped," boasted the middle brother called Gale, and noisily set out into the world bearing south.

He flew until he got to the edge of a village. There people had just finished threshing corn in one of the barns, and a peasant and his family were cleaning it, dividing the corn from the chaff.

Gale offered to help them.

"You're welcome," said the husbandman. "Then we shall be finished sooner." And so they were.

So powerfully did Gale blow into the granary that all the corn was at once scattered, the grains along with the chaff; even the sand from the threshing-floor was blown away as far as the opposite slope. Gale also blew off the roof of the barn, and carried it far away into the fields. The peasant lamented, cursed and threatened. And well he might! So much damage done: the corn gone, the barn roofless. Gale had to pay a ducat in gold as indemnity, otherwise the peasant would have lodged a complaint with the village mayor.

Afterwards Gale flew on towards the sea. There, in a harbour, fishermen were spreading the sails and getting ready to set out.

"I'll help you to sail out, fellows," Gale offered, and so strongly did he blow into the sails that he tore all of them off, and the boat rushed out like lightning. Before the cabin-boy could grip the rudder, the boat had run onto cliffs, and pierced its prow. The fishermen cursed the unwelcome helper, and made him pay a ducat as indemnity for the damage he had caused. Otherwise they threatened to bind him to a rock with a rope of steel so that he might do no more harm.

"Now I will try at the miller's," said Gale to himself. "He is sure to pay me well for blowing into the sails of his mill."

But even there he did not do too well. For no sooner had he applied his intractable breath to the sails than fragments were flying from them, and the mill was ruined.

The miller tore his hair in despair, but then he took hold of a branch of a birch tree and threatened to give Gale a sound thrashing unless he paid damages straight away. What was poor Gale to do? He gave him his last ducat, and set out for home empty-handed.

The king sadly shook his head when his middle son told him about his misfortunes and said, "Gale, I am sure you meant well. Only you don't know your strength, and so you had to pay the price for your ignorance."

Then Wind, the eldest of the brothers, set out into the world. He got to a village on the very first day. There, too, peasants had just finished threshing wheat, and the whole family was outside the barn cleaning the grain.

Wind bowed down to the threshing-floor, blew gently, and all the chaff flew off behind the barn like swarms of little flies. After this, all the husbandman had to do was to fill one sack after another with clean grain. They laboured hard until the evening. When their work was done a whole year's harvest stood in sacks ready for the mill.

"I'll take it to the mill tomorrow. And many thanks to you, Wind. But for your help we should have taken more than a week," said the farmer, and he rewarded Wind with a golden ducat.

Wind set out again on his travels. The next day he saw a fisherman's boat on the open sea. The men were rowing with all their might, but the boat was hardly moving. Indeed, it seemed to stand still. So Wind blew, the fishermen quickly drew out the sails, and before evening fell, they safely reached the harbour with their load. Overjoyed, they gave Wind two ducats for lending them a hand.

The third day, Wind came flying to the knoll where the windmill stood. The sails of the mill were hanging flabby and calm. Every now and then the careworn miller ran out to the top of the hill to look at the sky to see whether a whiff of wind might not blow from some quarter after all.

Wind rose and made the sails of the mill turn. He blew all day so that the miller managed to grind flour for the whole village, enough to last them all winter. He was pleased, and at parting gave Wind three ducats for helping him all day.

Wind returned home, and happily shook out all the gold coins before his royal father, those he had received from him as well as the others, and recounted how he had earned them.

The king commended him and said to his sons, "You have seen for yourselves which of you is the best husbandman. Therefore I have decided to hand over my Kingdom of Snow and the crystal palace to you, Wind. I am sure you are going to be a wise and just ruler."

Gale, offended, turned on his heel, and rushed out headlong. Ever since, he has flown frantically about the world because he has no home.

Blizzard has grown a bit wiser after the thrashing. From time to time he rushes out into the world, freezes lakes and rivers, or blows crisp snow onto the hills so that children may go skating, tobogganing and skiing. When he has heard them shouting with delight, he is content to return to the Kingdom of Snow.

The Magic Table

Once upon a time there lived an old barrel-maker. He was in poor health, and no longer did much work, and so he often had hardly a crust of bread to keep him from starving. One day a friend living on the other side of the forest remembered him, and asked the old man to make him a big kneading-trough. In return he promised him as much bread as he could carry, and a little money.

The old man got to work and it was not long before he put on the last hoops.

"Well, I can still do a good job of work," he said happily when he had finished, but his good mood did not last long: "How am I, a poor old man, to carry the trough beyond the forest? Indeed, it's so heavy that I can hardly lift it."

The old man mused and mused all day long but there was nothing he could devise — yet he would have to take his handiwork to the neighbour somehow.

So he rose with the lark, and putting the trough on his back, set out towards the forest. At first he made some progress, but as the sun got hotter the old man found it hard going. He threw the trough off his shoulders, turned it upside down, crept under it, and was asleep before you could say Jack Robinson.

This happened just under the old oak where the paths and the byways used by all forest animals cross. After a while, a hare came running past, and no sooner did he spot the kneading-trough than he said, "What a large table, as if specially made for a feast — and empty. Well, I will wait here — where there is a table, there is bound to be a bite to eat sooner or later."

Before long a wolf came along. Seeing the hare seated on the trough, he asked, "What are you doing sitting on that table? Is it yours?"

"Nothing of the kind," rejoined the hare. "But where there is a table, there is bound to be a feast." And he just sat on.

"You may be right," agreed the wolf, and joined the hare in waiting for the feast.

So the two just sat staring across the clearing, twiddling their thumbs, until the fox came along.

"What are you two doing here?" she wanted to know. "And what a fine table you have got!"

The wolf replied, "We are waiting for a feast, can't you see? This table is bound to be prepared for a repast."

The fox was none too ready to believe that. "Well, I don't know," she said scratching her ear. "I hope there is no magic behind this. It is around this oak that the devils are supposed to swarm at night."

"How can you, who set such store by your cleverness, say such things? How can you believe such old wives' tales?" And the hare burst out laughing.

The fox, not wanting to appear stupid, said nothing. She jumped up on to the trough and made herself comfortable, wondering what would happen next.

This time, however, they did not twiddle their thumbs for long. After some crackling noises in the glade, the old bear came rolling along.

"What are you idling about here for? Why aren't you all at work?" he growled, the moment he saw the animals. But the hare, who happened to be unusually bold that day, at once volunteered:

"We're waiting for a feast. You can see the lovely table, can't you? Whoever has brought it here is bound to bring the food as well!"

Like the fox before him, the bear was none too enthusiastic. And since he was the oldest and the strongest among animals, his decision was sure to be respected by one and all. He spoke harshly to the hare:

"Stuff and nonsense! No one has ever brought me anything to eat yet, I have always had to earn my keep. But since the table is here, let's prepare a feast ourselves! Each of you shall bring the best he can, and don't linger anywhere!"

So everyone set out to look for something to eat, only the fox muttering under her breath about the peculiar table and the devils.

Not long after this they met under the oak again. They had all managed to get dainties just suited for a feast: the wolf brought a fat sheep, the fox a goose, the bear a few honeycombs full of the sweetest honey, and the hare came under the oak rolling a head of juicy cabbage almost bigger than himself.

But no sooner did they lay their booty on the bottom of the upturned trough than a strange noise was heard from inside the table. The old man had woken up and turned on his side.

"Did you hear that?" cried the fox. "It's sure to be the devils swarming out of the earth under the table, I knew it, I knew it!"

The bear was about to hush the fox, because he had heard nothing himself, but at that moment the trough began to rise!

The animals waited no longer. Everybody dashed off as fast as their legs would carry them — and the hare fastest of all.

When finally the barrel-maker scrambled out into the light of day, and with a mighty yawn looked round, he could not believe his eyes. He had not even dreamed of such exquisite food for a long, long time, and now it was all his, even before he had delivered his work.

Well, this must be an enchanted spot, he decided, and quickly picked up the unexpected gifts to take them to his cottage.

A few days passed before the old man, having eaten his fill and fortified himself, managed to get the kneading-trough to his neighbour.

What his reward was this time, or how he fared after that, the fairy tale does not say. I only know that since those days the forest animals, being afraid of devils, avoided the old oak. The old man himself would come there every now and then to see if he would not find a new array of gifts. However, nothing — not even a toadstool — was seen to grow there ever again.

How the Poor Peasant Came to his Senses

Once upon a time, long, long ago, there lived in our village a wise husbandman. He was well aware that one evening he would lie down never to rise again. So when that day arrived, he summoned his only son and said to him, "My son, never be stingy and niggardly. Remember you will never be poor if you throw money about with full hands at the right time and in the right place."

Having said this, the old man closed his eyes, and grew sleepier and sleepier until he fell asleep for ever.

The son did not quite understand his father's legacy, and so he construed it in his own way. Knowing that every word spoken by his father was worth its weight in gold, he resolved to fulfil the old man's last wish as conscientiously as possible.

He chose the right time and the right place to do so.

He waited till the end of harvest, and afterwards raked together all the corn from his granary down to the last grain, and threw the lot into the river.

Hardly had the last grain dropped into the water than the surface rippled, and the Queen of the Waters with a golden crown on her head emerged. She smiled at the peasant and said in a soft sweet voice, "Good man, I will give you a rare gift for feeding all my fishes. From this day forward you will understand the speech of all birds and beasts. But mind you do not let anyone into the secret. If you ever disclose it to anybody, you may as well prepare your funeral."

The peasant bowed low to the lovely fairy, and set out for home. It was just noon, the sun was blazing mercilessly. For a while, he lay down in the shade under the linden-tree, shut his eyes and rested.

Suddenly, a crow with her offspring came flying there. They sat down upon a tree and started chatting together; and indeed, the peasant understood every word they were saying.

"Look, mother," said the little crow, "there is a dead man lying down there. I'll go and peck his eyes out."

But the old one warned her: "Don't be a fool, little one, he may not be dead, he may only be asleep."

"Never mind, I will try. Ma, you are always so terribly scared!"

She alighted on the sleeper, and pecked him carefully in the leg — nothing happened — he did not even budge. The young crow grew bold, jumped a little further, and pecked the man in the belly. And once again — nothing happened.

"You see, ma, he is dead as a doornail," crowed the little one in triumph, jumped still a little further until she sat on the man's chest, and was about to peck out his eye. Then, suddenly, snap! And the peasant held the rash young crow by the wing.

"Help, help, ma!" crowed the young one in despair.

"How can I help you now, you disobedient creature? If he would let you go,

I would take him to the golden treasure, but how am I to let him know?" crowed the old crow helplessly.

The peasant weighed her words and let the young crow go her way.

The old one crowed with joy, then they both flew a little distance to the forest. Once there, the old crow alighted on the ground, sat on a white round boulder under a fir-tree, and gave a long crowing sound:

"Here, here, here!"

The peasant came rushing there, rolled away the stone, and saw a thing such as he had never in his life seen before: among the roots of the fir-tree was a large earthen pot full of gold coins. He took the treasure home, bought all he needed, improved the farm, got married, and led a good and happy life.

One day, while he was passing the cowshed, he heard the goat and the ox talking together.

"Oh, dear, mine is a hard life!" moaned the ox. "You have no idea, Tuftchin, what drudgery it is to pull the plough from dawn to dusk."

The goat just grinned. "Why are you such a fool, my good old ox? Pretend to be ill, and you won't have to work!"

"You are right, Tuftchin, I'll try that tomorrow."

The next day the groom said to the farmer:

"The ox is ill, lying like dead on the straw. What shall we do?"

"That's bad luck. So put the goat to the plough and don't spare him, put him through his paces, he never does a spot of work," said the husbandman.

And that is what happened. The whole day the goat dragged the plough, his eyes sticking out with the strain, his hairs glued together with sweat and earth, his back smarting under the whip.

The sun had long set and he was still dragging the plough through the long furrows. It was dark, and the moon was shining like a gold coin, before the goat shambled into the shed.

"Well, how did you fare, old boy? What's the news?" the ox welcomed him good-heartedly.

"I am all right," said the goat. "I've got nothing to fear. But I hear the butcher is coming to fetch you tomorrow. 'What can we do with a sick ox,' the husbandman was heard to say. 'He doesn't pull any more, so we'll slaughter him and have his flesh smoked for winter.'"

"I'll be all right tomorrow," said the ox in fright.

The farmer heard the conversation, and could not help laughing. Still giggling, he came to the living room.

"What are you laughing at?" asked his wife, but the husband just waved his hand, and went on laughing. "Well, do tell me, so that I can have a laugh as well."

"Never you mind," said the man, and stopped laughing to avoid further questioning.

The wife, rather offended, put the dinner on the table. The man took some food and poured himself some tea. For a while he ate quietly, but suddenly he remembered the stupid ox and the sly goat, and he burst out laughing again until he nearly choked.

This was too much for the housewife. She grew angry, and insisted that her husband tell her what he was laughing about, saying she had a right to know. He must tell her without fail, or there would be trouble. But the husbandman waved her away: "Leave me alone now. I know you are curious like every woman, but I won't tell you!"

"But I want to know. I won't leave you alone until you tell me, I won't and I won't!"

The man stopped laughing. "Wife, be sensible, I can't tell you, it's a secret, and it would be my death, if I gave it away."

Of course, that was something he ought not have said, for it only served to excite the wife's curiosity. She kept silent for a while, but then she insisted with ever-increasing vehemence. Throughout the night she worried her husband with questions until at last, towards daybreak, he gave in.

"What can I do," he sighed, "if I don't confide my secret to the woman, she'll worry me to death with her curiosity. So I must tell her, and prepare for leaving this world."

And so the farmer told his wife the secret, and then made preparations for his own funeral.

First, he watered all the fruit trees in the orchard, pouring a pail of water on the roots of each. Then he cut a loaf of bread into pieces for the fowl and a smoked joint for the dogs, and poured out a full bowl of milk for the cats.

Then he had a hot bath, shaved his chin for the last time, trimmed his moustache, greased his hair, and combed it with a parting down the middle. He put on a long starched shroud, lay down on a board in the middle of the room, bade candles to be lit, and sent for the priest. His wife was ordered to brew a lot of beer and prepare a rich feast for the mourners.

A window was opened behind his head so that his soul might soar straight to heaven. And through that window a strange conversation was wafted to the husbandman.

"Cock, you should be ashamed of yourself," howled the sheep-dog from the kennel. "The landlord is dying on us, and here you go just picking out the fattest morsels as if nothing was the matter. How can you think of food?"

"And is there anything the matter?" the cock retorted. "You feed yourself as well, it will not happen again that the niggard should prepare a feast for us with his own hands!"

"What are you crowing about, you gossip-monger?" yelped the ginger dachshund. "The landlord has never been niggardly. True enough he used to be careful, but prudent and wise."

The cock put his legs apart, and crowed derisively.

"Nonsense — wise. Prudent — my foot! A reckless Jack that's what he has been. When his father on his death-bed advised him not to be niggardly, and be a spendthrift at the right time throwing about his goods with full hands, what he meant was that he should be generous and hand out bread to the poor when bad harvest and hunger descend upon the land. And what did he do? He threw all the harvest into the river with his own hands, that fool of a farmer!"

"Well, all right. Let bygones be bygones. He must have been well aware what he was doing, for he is the master of the house," pleaded the ginger dachshund for his landlord.

"He — master of the house? Ha ha ha! You must be joking, doggie. Our master has always played the second fiddle. It is his foolish wife whose word counts here, and he only dances to the tune she pipes! Indeed, at this very moment he is preparing to die only to be rid of her old-womanish curiosity!"

"The cock is right," said a sweet soft voice beside the husbandman. It was the lovely Queen of the Waters with the golden crown on her head who had appeared out of the blue, and stood smiling at the stunned man in the shroud.

"You have given away our secret, which you should not have done. To atone for this, you have arranged your own funeral, and that is enough. Indeed, I will not let you die because of a foolish woman's curiosity! Just go on living happily, but from this day you shall not understand what the animals say to each other."

Having said this, the Queen of the Waters turned into a rosy little cloud, and floated out through the open window.

The farmer laughed merrily, and jumped straight off the bier. First, he blew out the burial candles, then he quickly got rid of the shroud, and put on his Sunday best. He invited the neighbours, relatives, and all poor people from the whole neighbourhood, and gave not a burial feast but such a banquet that the merry feasting was the talk of the whole district for a long time to come.

Nor was the cock forgotten. The farmer treated him to a full bowl of sunflower seeds. Let him enjoy the feast, for he has deserved it, the clever bird!

road, and pick at will with her beak the lovely thick caterpillars from the cabbage in the little garden. Most of all, she missed her buddy Darkgrey. How happy she had been chatting and playing with him!

Poor Piping-hen was pining away with sorrow; her feathers lost their lustre, the crest on her sad little head gradually lost its clear red colour, the merry sparks in her eyes dying down one after another. The golden eggs she laid grew smaller and smaller, until one day she laid none at all.

What a commotion there was then! The old man wanted to send for the doctor. Or perhaps they had better get the hen a new cage, one made of gold?

The old woman shouted her husband down. "You have gone utterly mad. Why buy a golden cage for the ungrateful fowl? She is not at all badly off with us, is she? She has an entire parlour to herself, and a silver cage. She is admired by everybody. And this is how the ungrateful creature repays our care!"

She paused to catch her breath, and then went on, "What are we to do with her now that she has stopped laying eggs? Doctor, my foot! The cook should be called. When she is no longer willing to lay golden eggs, on to the frying pan with her!"

At once she called the cook, and ordered him to cut the hen's throat and bake her with chestnut stuffing.

But there she made a great mistake.

The cook came, opened the silver cage, seized the sorrowful hen, and was about to carry her to the kitchen.

The hen cackled in despair:

> "Cockle-doodle-doo,
> My dear friend Darkgrey, where are you?
> Dear Darkgrey, can you hear my cry?
> I'm being carried off to fry."

The tomcat heard his friend crying for help, and was down from the loft in one jump. He stole silently up to the cook from behind, jumped on to his back and plunged his sharp claws into the fat scruff of the man's neck. The cook cried out with pain, put his hands to his neck, and ran away. The hen spread her wings, and flew out through the open window. The tomcat jumped out after her, and once again they were out in the courtyard together as old friends, just as before.

And indeed, everything around them was as it had been, as though somebody had waved a magic wand. On the very same site where only a little while before the splendid mansion had stood, there was the old ramshackle hovel with the small courtyard where Piping-hen was rooting in the ashes.

The old table with its table-cloth still stands in the corner of the tiny room with a single egg lying on it. The old woman is getting ready to fry the egg on her little pan, the moment the old man has made a fire in the oven.

This time the tomcat will not smash the egg, because he is dozing contentedly on the oven. There is a faint smile playing on his lips. Perhaps he is dreaming of the time when he and Piping-hen are going to have a chat and a game again.

ing, and go on singing until the evening. People delight in the Sun's rays, the world is full of radiant light, brilliance and good cheer. But when the Sun sets, it looks as though life on Earth had ceased and gone out altogether.

This is something I must put right, resolved the Creator, and his face lit up. There must be light in the night as well! He went on musing for a while, and then he called Ilmarin, his favourite helper, and addressed him as follows:

"Ilmarin, it is not long since you succeeded in vaulting the canopy of Heaven above the Earth. That, indeed, was a master's work. What you should do now is to hang upon this magnificent vault some light that would illumine the Earth when the Sun has laid himself down to rest. Darkness is not a good thing, it only makes men sad."

Ilmarin, the heavenly blacksmith, understood the Creator's intention, and without much pondering set to work.

First, he directed his steps to the Silver Mountain and cut off a whole side of it with his mighty hammer. Then he fired a giant forge, and filled it with all the mined silver ore he had. When it had melted, he seized his sledge-hammer again, and beat it into an enormous silver orb, not unlike a gigantic mill-wheel. Next he put a golden, thinly hammered cover upon it. Finally came his most exacting task — to set inside the orb a bright cold fire to illuminate his work from inside when darkness descended on all things.

Being a good husbandman, Ilmarin went round the smithy picking up the dispersed chips of gold plating that were left over, and used them to hammer out an infinite number of stars of varying sizes. He polished them to make them shine, and assigned each of them a fixed place in the sky. After this, he let the Moon out on to the canopy of Heaven, and determined his course so as not to cross, but to alternate with the course of the Sun.

This was the start of a new life on Earth. As soon as the Sun had sunk below the horizon, the Moon sailed out silently on the other side, lighting up the whole sleeping landscape with his silvery twilight. All around him the countless stars glittered faintly showing him the way through the dark of the night. At the end of their heavenly journeyings the Moon and his starry retinue laid themselves down to rest somewhere in the soft waves of the ocean. At that moment the Sun sailed out on the opposite side of the sky and took over the job of making men, birds, beasts, trees and flowers happy with his light.

Thus everybody had enough light at night as well as in daytime. People were happy, and magnified the Creator for having arranged everything so wisely.

However, do as you may, you can't please everybody! There were some malcontents who found it very distressing that the nights were no longer steeped in darkness, for now people could easily see them when they were up to some mischief.

And Hell was in an uproar, too. Lucifer and his mob were mad with the Creator for having brought light into night's darkness. How would they now manage to catch people? Thieves and robbers now crept by night like cats, but this was of no use to the devils. Men always caught sight of them, and then the evil-doers were in for it, and were punished by the people themselves. And what was then left over for them, the devils? They often spent whole night rummaging among people, yet now they had no chance of ensnaring a single sinner!

So great misery descended upon the devils. Hell became a place of want, hunger and dissatisfaction. The devils were gloomy and sullen.

Lucifer saw he had to do something to stop the Moon from shining. However, he did not know how to go about it. So he called all the devils together for a conference. More minds, more sense, he said to himself, but came to regret it.

No sooner had the devils gathered than Hell became as noisy as a running mill. They were all talking, one above the other, and each felt how extremely important he was. Yet there was one thing they all agreed upon: the Moon was their enemy, because he illuminated all nooks and corners by night, and he should be absolutely effaced from the vault of Heaven. Otherwise all devils would perish from want and humiliation.

"Well, all right, there we are! But how we can get the silver busybody off the sky, that is what nobody can tell me," mused Lucifer in great irritation.

So the horned lot went on conferring with one another until the close of the seventh day, when they were so hungry they had a rumbling in their bowels. Lucifer wound up the unending debate and made the following decision:

"Darkness is what we devils need for our work, and moonshine is bad for us. The best thing would be to eliminate the Moon from the vault of Heaven, but how is this to be done? It is impossible to drag him down by the legs, and he can't be caught in a net. He would be much too big a fish to catch! So what we must do is to scramble up to him, and paint him over with tar. This we shall do when he rises above our forest in the evening. He will be in his lowest elevation. We have tar galore in Hell, and Beelzebub and his sons will make a long ladder. But mind you, the ladder must be at least seven times as high as the highest tree in the forest. Only when we have blackened the Moon's silver face will that kind and cosy darkness of ours return to the Earth."

The devils gave their leader a stormy round of applause for having devised things so cleverly, and set to work without delay. By evening the immensely long ladder was ready, and no sooner had the silvery Moon swung up over the forest than the devils leant the ladder against the nearest tree. Two of the boldest devils climbed up on it. One carried a big shaggy brush, the other a pail full of tar, and at once they set to work: one did the painting, the other held up the pail for him to dip the brush in the tar. But the Moon kept rising across the sky, so the devils had to climb higher and higher, one rung after the other. When they reached the last rung, the upper devil said:

"It's no good, mate. I must climb up on the moon; I'll get a hold on him somehow, and then you pass me the pail and the brush. When I have blackened over that silvery Easter-cake, I'll jump down somewhere, I hope."

And that is what they did. The upper devil swung up onto the Moon's edge, fixed his pail there, and painted the Moon's shining face over bit by bit with thick black tar.

The devils gathered down by the forest jumped about like goats, yelling for joy, smacking their shanks, and crying at the top of their voices:

explained the old devil. "In the morning they get up and cross themselves, every one of them, they say their prayers before breakfast, they say grace before and after lunch, before dinner and after dinner, before going to bed, and they constantly cross themselves..."

"Stop babbling about people crossing themselves!" shouted Beelzebub angrily.

"And what nice names they use in addressing each other!" went on the old devil, nothing daunted: "All you hear is: dear Daddy, dear Mummy, dear grandpa, dear granny, dear auntie, dear brother-in-law and so on. No one would even dream of swearing. These people don't seem to know a single sinful word."

"I should like to see this saintly family with my own eyes," said Beelzebub.

The two went on quarrelling for a long time. The other devils mostly joined Beelzebub's side, claiming that there was no man on Earth so perfect he would not commit at least one sin. But the old devil insisted that this family was a true paragon of purity and integrity.

Of course, the argument could only end in a wager. Devils are keen on betting at the slightest provocation.

So they bet each other a kettle of hellish brandy that in three days Beelzebub would have tempted one member of that family and made him at least swear. It was agreed that even such a slight sin would be enough for him to win.

Early in the morning of the next day Beelzebub set out to tempt the people in that farmstead. No sooner had he looked round than he realized that the old devil was probably right.

Everything in the farmstead was nice, clean and tidy, the house spick and span, the courtyard like a little chamber. The landlord, the landlady, relatives, children and servants were all trim and neat as if on holiday. They were hardworking, gentle, talking affably to each other, and no one gave anyone so much as a bad look.

"Well, we shall see!" growled Beelzebub, and set his first trap for grandfather, who was mowing the meadow behind the farmstead: what he did was to put an old brick under a tuft of clover. Grandpa mowed merrily along, entirely unaware of the trap, and swung his scythe — till clang! his scythe broke in two.

"Oh dear, what a clumsy fellow I am!" lamented Grandpa, and burst into tears — such a sharp and handy little scythe it had been!

"Don't be upset, dear Grandpa," the husbandman tried to comfort him as he passed by with a loaded waggon. "I will bring you a new scythe in a moment." Thus the first day Beelzebub did not carry it off. The next day he sat a trap for the husbandman. As the latter was bringing in a full load of aftergrass, one wheel fell off suddenly, and the waggon overturned.

"Oh dear, what bad luck! Dear children, dear brother-in-law, please come and help me!" cried the farmer, and all he did was to shake his head thoughtfully. "I thought this might happen, I should have exchanged that old linchpin long ago. You always have to pay the price for negligence."

So once again Beelzebub's trap did not work. On the third day, he set a trap for grandmother. "She is very old now, and is sure to remember her young days when people could swear with great gusto whenever something they were doing misfired. You wait and see, old woman, how I am going to make you swear!" said Beelzebub to himself, and set to work.

He waited for her to come out into the courtyard to strew grain to the fowls. Then he quickly turned into a hawk, circled round the flock, picked out the best hen, and carried her off in his claws before the old woman's nose.

The old woman dropped the osier basket, the grain scattered, the fowls dispersed around the whole courtyard. Then she wrung her wrinkled hands, and whispered sadly, "God's will be done. Glorified be his name."

Hearing the grandmother say this, Beelzebub spat three times. He was really at his wits' end. What was he to do with these people? There was nothing for it. What a pity! He had lost his bet and that kettle of hellish brandy.

So he set out along a narrow forest path back to Hell. At the crossroads he met a woman selling medicinal herbs. There was something peculiar about her, she was neither young nor old, and her eyes shone out from under her shawl like those of a weasel.

"What's the matter, sir, why are you so sadly loitering?" she inquired.

I will tell her about my trouble, at least it will be a relief, Beelzebub decided and told the woman all about what ailed him. The sorceress thought for a while, then her eyes lit up, and she said, "I know of a remedy. But what will you give me if I help you?" The devil instantly recovered his good spirits, and promised wonders to the herbalist if only she would help him.

"Well, all right," said the woman. "At noon you can come to the farm, and you shall hear with your own ears how those hypocrites are going to thunder their curses. But remember: Even though you win the wager you shall not carry off any sinning soul with you. That wouldn't be just."

Willy-nilly Beelzebub agreed, and suggested striking a bargain. But the woman stopped him: "Wait a moment, I haven't told you yet what you must give me in return for the little service. I demand white kidskin gloves long up to the elbows and black patent-leather boots up to the knees. Is it a deal?"

Beelzebub, having the power to conjure up anything for anyone, was only too ready to accept such a deal. And so, having agreed on that, the two of them parted.

The woman set out at once for the farmhouse. The only person she found there was the farmer's wife, and she begged a piece of bread from her. At once the housekeeper made her heartily welcome, asking her to sit down at the table, and giving her plenty to eat and drink. The herbalist thanked her for all the good things, and as she was leaving asked the farmer's wife in confidence if her husband was still in love with her.

"Why, of course! You wouldn't believe how much," laughed the farmer's wife, but the woman persisted, "Well, all right. But it used to be better when you were young, am I not right?"

"You know, madam, the older you get, the more work and cares you have to worry you, and so you don't even think of other things," admitted the house-keeper.

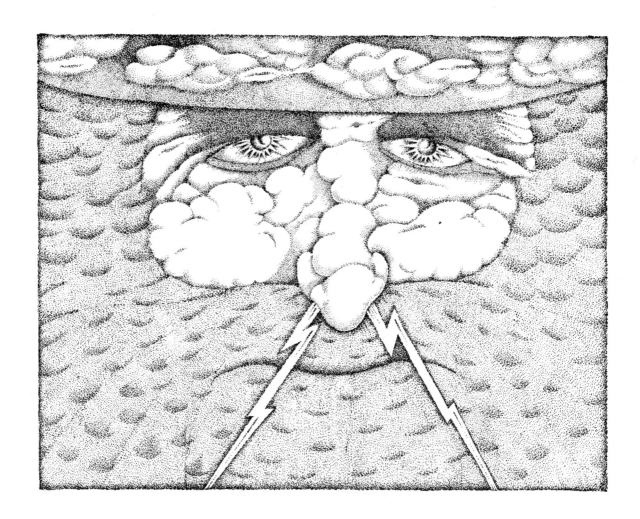

How the Bricklayer
Outwitted the Devil

The bricklayer's job is not an easy one. All day long he stands on the scaffolding, breathing in the dust from the bricks and the lime, with the sun burning hot and mercilessly scorching, so that by the evening he is as dry as a cod. No wonder he is always thirsty.

On one particular day Ans the bricklayer had to quench his thirst properly in the local inn. Many a tankard had he poured down his parched throat before he finally set out for home. No wonder he was swung about from side to side like the washing on the line when it is thrown about by the wind. He took the wrong path, and ended up in the churchyard. There he stumbled against the kerbstone of a freshly dug grave, and fell straight in. Actually, it turned out to be not a grave but a deep pit. Ans dropped lower and lower until all of a sudden he found himself in Hell.

Having had several falls from the scaffolding, he was not unduly scared. The devils, taken up with their hellish avocations, paid no attention to him. Some were carrying firewood, others were putting it on the fire, still others were stirring something in the big cauldrons, and those who happened to be off duty were sitting at a table playing cards.

The bricklayer surveyed Hell with curiosity, but then he started wondering how he could get out of there and back to Earth. After a while he grinned — he had a brain-wave!

Everybody knows that a proper bricklayer always carries a leather bag slung over his shoulder containing the most essential bricklayer's tools. So Ans put his hand in the bag, and took out his folding yard-measure and bricklayer's hammer.

Then he set about making some measurements in the hall and driving a peg here and there with his hammer. Lucifer on his sulphur throne being in his way, he moved him to the back wall, and went on surveying. With a big carpenter's pencil he put down some numbers in his notebook, gave the ceiling a searching look, and nodded contentedly.

It was only then that the devils began to take notice of the strange fellow, wondering what he might be surveying down in Hell. Lucifer thundered at Ans sullenly:

"What are you hopping about for with that measure, you clown?"

"No clown, sir! I am a bricklayer," rejoined Ans calmly, "and am sent here by His Grace our bishop to build a church in these parts. So I must take measurements for the foundations."

"Fie, fie," whimpered the devils in a chorus, and started spitting into the fire till it hissed like a regiment of vipers, probably to ward off the terrible news about the building of a church.

"Have you got any sense, man?" growled Lucifer. "Whoever has heard of it — a church in Hell?! Has that bishop of yours got bats in his belfry?"

"Oh no, he hasn't," said the bricklayer calmly. "His Grace our bishop is a wise and saintly man. He says there should be a church in every hole, and that's why he has sent me down here."

Now the devils saw that things were beginning to look bad. First, they tried in a friendly way to persuade the bricklayer to give up the survey. Then they wanted to bribe him, and pushed hot chestnuts into his pockets, but in vain. Ans deliberately went on with his surveying work: here he drove in a peg, there he scratched a groove in the floor with his bricklayer's hammer.

In the end, Lucifer lost his temper, and jumping up from his throne and catching the bricklayer by the neck, threw him out through the same hole he had dropped in.

And so Ans found himself in the churchyard again and was happy to have got out of Hell so easily. Only he had two bumps on his forehead, which he had picked up in the narrow hole when Lucifer threw him out so savagely.

This time the bricklayer did not lose his way. He went straight to the local inn, for his throat had gone thoroughly dry again in Hell's heat.

There in the tap-room he sat down among his companions, and he felt free and easy and in a happy mood. After a while, however, his comrades started laughing at him, saying he smelt of sulphur, and one joker went so far as to yell out, "Look, neighbours, he's got horns coming out of his forehead! I bet our Ans is chumming with the devil!"

Everyone burst out laughing, but Ans frowned, drank up, paid his bill, and went home. He was livid with Lucifer because of the bumps, for they put him to shame and made him a laughing stock.

I will pay you back for this, Hell's ruler! said the bricklayer to himself.

On the following Sunday he prepared a feast in his house, and invited all his relatives and friends from far and near. Lucifer was also invited, and so was the thunderer from the mountains with whom the bricklayer had drunk many a tumbler in the tap-room in good companionship.

He knew that the thunderer — who was sometimes called Thunderclap — was no lover of devils. This went back to the time when one of them had stolen Thunderclap's bagpipes, on the day when a great thunderstorm shook the mountains.

That day, Thunderclap was so tired that he dozed off in the fields, his bagpipes by his side. A devil who happened to be loitering about took a fancy to the bagpipes, and resolved to steal them. Thunderclap had been careful enough to put one hand on his bagpipes before going to sleep. If the devil tried to pull them out, however carefully, the Ruler of the Mountains was sure to wake up, and the devil would certainly come to harm. But being sly as a fox, the devil knew at once what to do. He caught a well-fed louse in his pitchy head of hair, and threw it under Thunderclap's shirt. After a while the louse, having settled in its new surroundings, went busily to work. Thunderclap could not but scratch himself. The moment he lifted his hand, the devil grabbed the bagpipes and made off, leaving only the smell of sulphur behind him. And it was that smell of his that gave him away as the one who had robbed the thunderer of his bagpipes. Thunderclap has hated all devils ever since.

The thunderer loved a good party, and the bricklayer's party was one of the best. After a while, the wine went to Thunderclap's head, he became merry, and started playing various pranks in his own manner: He waved his right arm — and there was lightning; he waved his left arm — and it thundered till the pictures dropped from the walls. The devil took fright, and crept under the table, trembling with fear. Then the thunderer clapped his hands, and the table collapsed. Lucifer, all terrified, went white as a sheet, and begged the bricklayer to hide him.

"Jump out of the window! There is a haystack outside the cottage. Just crawl in, nobody will find you there," Ans advised the devil in a low voice, but at the same time he was laughing inside.

The devil followed the bricklayer's advice. He flew out of the window head forward, and landed straight in the haystack with only a little piece of his tail showing.

Meanwhile, the merry thunderer was full of pranks to show off before the neighbours, who were used to his ways, and loved his tricks.

He snorted — and sparks flew from his nose; he sneezed, and there was a roll of thunder; he spat into the corner — and lightning crossed the sky. They were all amazed, and applauded him with great enthusiasm.

"That's nothing," boasted Thunderclap. "Fetch the little cannon I left in the hall. Then you'll see something really worth seeing!"

So, anxious to see some fun, they pulled the cannon into the room.

"Where shall I shoot?" asked the thunderer.

"Why not through the window into that haystack outside the cottage, if you can hit it?" suggested the cunning bricklayer already rubbing his hands with satisfaction.

"How could I miss it!" boasted Thunderclap, took aim and fired.

There was a terrific discharge, and the whole house jumped in its foundations.

When the smoke cleared, the haystack with Lucifer in it had disappeared.

Nobody knows how he fared, whether the cannon-ball blew him to smithereens, or whether he flew with the hay up into the sky and got stuck somewhere among the clouds. God only knows what really happened.

A Good Man

Once upon a time there was a magic lake in the woods far away. Like a small sea its waves rolled through the countryside, and on its shore, close to the road leading to the fishing village, stood the little hut of a solitary old man.

It was not much he needed for his living. Now and then he caught a fish, sometimes a hare or a little rabbit got trapped in his snare. The old man spent most of his time weaving hemp into ropes and cables. This was hard toil, and his hands hardened from doing it, but the old man was content, although he knew rope-making would never make him rich. Truth to tell, he never coveted riches.

One day three hunters stopped at his hut. For a while they watched the old man at his toil, and felt sorry for him. And they bought from him more ropes than they really needed. All he wanted for the lot were three little copper coins, but they gave him three gold ducats.

"What shall I do with so much money?" said the old man in dismay. "I don't need them at all, you know."

"Don't turn them down, grandpa," said one of the hunters coaxingly. "When you have money, you can afford to have a little rest. You have done enough work in your life."

But the old man would not dream of resting.

No sooner did the hunters leave than he fetched an armful of hemp from the loft and, having wetted and combed it thoroughly, he started weaving a new rope. Then he remembered the ducats, and put them behind the band of his hat which he had never taken off in his life.

But then a strange thing happened.

When he finished his work and was washing in the courtyard, he put his hat on the edge of the well. The magpie, allured by the glitter of one of the ducats that showed behind the band, alighted on the well, seized the hat with her claws, and before the old man recovered from his surprise, she was gone.

The old man waved a threatening hand towards the forest where the magpie had flown, and murmured, "You confounded little thief!"

He was not so very sad about the loss of the money. What grieved him was the loss of his hat, which had done him faithful service for more than thirty years.

The very next day he set about a new job of work again. He started weaving an enormous fishermen's net. When it was ready, he called the fishermen from the village, and handed his handiwork to them. The fishermen were glad to have the new net. They really needed one by then, but had little money — all they scrounged together was two small groats. The old man did not take any money from them, for they were even poorer than he was.

He also added a long rope for repairs, but the fishermen showed some hesitation in accepting the gift.

"If you won't have it otherwise," said the old man in the end, "bring me some little fish from the first haul you make with this new net."

The fishermen agreed, and immediately set out on their fishing expedition. They threw the new net into the lake, and when they hauled it out, there was but a single fish fluttering in it — an enormous pike.

They brought it to the old man — his table was hardly big enough to hold it.

As could be expected, the old man at once began cooking it. When gutting the fish, he found a magnificent glittering diamond in its belly. He laid it on his palm, but had to veil his eyes quickly with the other hand — so strong was the light radiated by the diamond!

At that moment high waves rose on the lake, and the Lady of the Lake in a silver robe emerged. The long golden tresses of her golden hair fell down on her shoulders. She directed her dancing steps towards the old man, and her soft voice sounded like a flute: "Old man, the diamond you are holding in your hand was pried by that thief of a pike out of our King of the Lake's crown. Now the king will not have the disfigured crown put on his head, and without a crown he is unable to reign! Therefore he sends you word to return that diamond to him. In return he offers you a fishing boat filled up to the brim with gold ducats."

"What would I do with so much money?" asked the old man, astonished.

"The King of the Lake knows that you are not greedy, that you have never coveted money. He will fulfil any wish you may have, if you return the precious stone to him," begged the Lady of the Lake in her sweet voice.

"Here you are, lovely nymph, accept the stone from the lake crown. I do not need it," said the old man, and added after a moment's thought, "If, however, His Majesty insists on rewarding somebody, it is our fishermen who deserve it. After all, it was they who fished out the pike-thief. You are sure to have seen their wretched hovels in the village. Let the King of the Lake have new little houses built for them. What do you think, can he manage to do that?"

"Of course, he can, that I can promise you," smiled the Lady of the Lake sweetly, hiding the precious diamond in her bosom. "But what should our king do for you, old man?"

Again he thought for a while, then he lowered his eyes, blushed, and said in a timid low voice, "As for myself, I would need, if this were possible, to make my shed a bit larger so that I might make longer ropes in it."

"It shall be done!" said the Lady of the Lake in her sweet voice clear as bell, and entered the lake, whose surface rippled just a trifle.

The next morning, as the old man stepped out in front of his cottage, he thought he was seeing a vision, and could not believe his eyes.

Where only the day before the wretched fishermen's hovels had huddled together, there were now pretty white cottages and houses shining in straight rows. The fishing village had been turned into a little town overnight.

His own dwelling, too, looked brand new, and all across the courtyard down to the nearby forest extended the new rope-maker's workshop. At once the old man stalked with a firm step through the long workshop till he reached its end.

He looked towards the forest, and what did he see?

On the nearest birch there was a magpie's nest, and in it — wonder of wonders! — his beloved old black hat. Immediately, he ran home to fetch a long pole, and pulled the hat down. Behind the tattered band there still glittered the three gold ducats he had received from the kind hunters some time before.

The old man had enough money now. Anyone else in his situation would have taken a rest. But he still had his busy skilful hands, and they would not let him be idle. And besides, he now had that brand new shed! And there he twisted hemp into lovely long ropes for a long time.

And the little town that grew up overnight on the shore of that magic lake stands there to this day, and is said to be growing bigger and prettier from year to year.

How the Devil Learnt to Snore

Far and wide over the meadows the haymaking season set in, and there was need for every willing hand. Even the poorest man could make his living by mowing the grass, and if you were not much good at mowing, you could always try your hand at haymaking.

Though one has to work for many a long day before the dried hay is stored in the hayloft, haymaking is no drudgery. Even the eternally sleepy idler called Brencis, who had no other skill except snoring, which he did with a true saw-cutting noise, decided to help in the fields. But then something surprising happened. One night, Brencis was fast asleep. His snoring caught the attention of a visitor from Hell who was still a greenhorn among devils. He had been sent to knock about the world and gather experience, and to learn some sense, in which he was sorely deficient. When this young devil crept out of Hell's hole and heard Brencis snore, he was seized by the desire to learn whose mouth it was that produced such enchanting sounds.

As it happened, Brencis was at his very best that night. He was lying on his back on the sweet-smelling hay, entirely oblivious of the world around him, snoring so hard that the rafters positively rattled above him. The young devil ran about in the dark, throwing light on Brencis from his glowing eyes, and sighing with admiration.

Perhaps the devil inadvertently touched the fellow, or perhaps Brencis dreamed that he was chasing a cat. For he suddenly stretched out his arm, and caught the poor little devil by the tail.

What a surprise it was for both of them! Brencis was all but dead when he woke up at last to find himself holding a living devil in his hand. To his amazement the imp was mild, not to say humble. Far from raising Hell, he begged Brencis to take him on as an apprentice, adding he would make it worth his while should the master condescend to teach him.

"Cut the cackle. Is it haymaking you want me to teach you?" asked Brencis, stunned by the devil's request.

The devil shook his head. "Haymaking is child's play. What I should like to learn is your wonderful art of snoring. Not even Beelzebub can snore like that, and I am sure it will make me more esteemed in Hell..."

What a stupid little fellow this is, thought Brencis to himself, but what he said was: "All right, if you insist, I will try to teach you how to snore. Fortunately, I haven't got too many pupils at the moment. But mind you, it will cost you no less than this cap full of ducats." And he showed him his old ragged cap.

"I will be only too glad to pay, bud I can't bring you a capful of ducats all at once," said the devil sadly. "Young devils don't get so much money in Hell, you know, but I am certain to scrounge the money together in a month's time. And so that you may believe me, I can make hay for you throughout that month."

Brencis acted though as he were pondering the offer.

Finally he said, "I can't say I like the way the devil, of all creatures, is obliged to haggle, but what am I to do with you? Mind you bring at least a substantial handful by the morning. As for the haymaking, I take you at your word. Now be gone and let me go to sleep." So saying, Brencis lay down again and snored to his heart's content.

The devil would have been delighted to listen to him until dawn, but he had to go back to Hell to fetch the ducats lest the master should change his mind about taking him on.

He was back before dawn. Brencis was still breathing heavily, so he began to jingle the gold coins about his ears.

"What the devil is going on now?" asked the sleeper, opening one of his eyes.

"I have brought you ten ducats!" boasted the horned one. "At least you can see that the devil keeps his word. And when will you start with your teaching?"

"After you have turned the hay on the whole meadow. Don't you dare come before you have done," rejoined Brencis, and fell asleep again.

What was the devil to do? He toiled with the rake in the sun all day, while all Brencis did was lie about in the hayloft. Only in the evening did he let the devil in, and told him, "Now I am going to sleep again. When you hear me snore, try to do it after me. But don't disturb me before you have really learnt something."

So Brencis lay down on his back, shut his eyes, and a while later the devil was able to start learning. However, unable to lie on his back, he crouched like a cat, taking the deepest breaths he could, but what came out was far short of real snoring. It was just as if mice were rustling in the hayloft.

In the end, the devil, aggrieved and tired after the whole day's toil, fell asleep. But he determined to be more attentive the next day; he would be damned if he should not learn from Brencis how to snore!

The imp was really determined, but the second day everything went as before, and the third day was the same as the second. The ducats in the cap were pleasantly multiplying, and the hay was all swept together into haycocks.

And so it went. Once or twice he thought he had learnt something and woke up Brencis, but Brencis only laughed at him. "Why do you bother me with such whimpering? Is this what I have been trying to teach you?"

A whole month passed without the devil improving even slightly. On the other hand, the cap was full of ducats, the hay had been made, and Brencis went about with a broad smile on his face.

"You at least ought to return those ducats to me since I haven't learnt any snoring from you," said the devil reproachfully when the last day arrived.

This time Brencis took some pity on the foolish and inexperienced goblin. "You have learnt nothing because you are a dunce," he said. "That's why I am not going to return any money to you. All I can give you is a piece of good advice: Don't make the same mistake ever again."

"So what would you advise me to do?" asked his disciple.

"A devil can never learn how to snore. It is possible only when you lie on your back, and that is what you can't do because of your tail. The only thing you could do, if you were really serious, would be to cut the tail off, and become a normal man."

What the imp decided to do I don't pretend to know. What I do know is that Brencis was always happy to remember him, since thanks to the devil's ducats he was able to idle away his time in prosperity as long as he lived.

The Cock and the Thief

Once upon a time, there lived a man who was so poor that he had not even a dry crust left to eat. He resolved to go to his rich neighbour, and beg him to help him out. The neighbour was a notorious miser. When the poor man had gone down on his knees, his big-bellied neighbour condescendingly gave him one bean, but added a piece of good advice: "Put the bean in water for half a day, it will swell, and then you can boil soup for yourself to last maybe for two days."

The poor man put the bean in his cap, thanked him, and went sadly home. When he was about to throw it into the pot with water in it, the bean spoke to him in a soft human voice: "Please, man, do not eat me! You would not appease your hunger with a single bean anyway. Plant me in the garden, and you will see what I shall grow into in three days."

The poor man was amazed at the bean's speech, but did as the bean had bidden him. He planted it in his garden in a shaded place, watered it, and waited. When he came to the garden on the third day, he could hardly believe his eyes. The bean had grown into a high stalk wrapped round with thick pods, and its top was lost in the clouds.

The poor man first picked the pods as far up as he could reach. He shelled them, and immediately returned a whole bag of beans to the niggardly neighbour. The latter neither showed surprise, nor gave any thanks. The next day, the poor man used a ladder and climbed high into the crown of the beanstalk, and there, on the very top, which was nearly lost in the clouds, he saw something magically beautiful — a large rosy shell. It shone there like a star.

"How did that magnificent thing get up there?" gasped the astonished man. Then he took the shell down carefully and put it to his ear. But what he heard was not the roar of ocean waves. The only sound coming out of the shell was that same soft, gentle little voice: "Take me home with you, I will bring you luck. When you are in need, shake me three times: but don't do this if you have enough of everything."

As if in a dream, the man climbed down the bean stalk, brought the shell to his room, and being at once curious and in need, he shook it three times over the table, whereupon an unprecedented thing happened: what dropped out of the shell were golden ducats!

The poor man stood there dumbfounded. He hid the miraculous shell in his larder, picked up the gold coins, and bought enough food with them to last him all the winter.

The next day, he shook the shell again three times, counted the coins, and went to the market to buy a cow, some sheep and a ram. Afterwards he drove to the saw-mill to buy boards, which he used to repair his leaking roof and shed.

The rich neighbour saw all this, came to see him, and inquired where the poor man had suddenly got so much money. He pestered him with questions until the poor man showed him his magic shell. Of course, the rich man envied him, and wanted to buy it from him.

"Just say how much you want for it, and I will set down the money here on the spot."

"Go away," laughed the poor man. "This shell is definitely not for sale."

So they did not strike a bargain, and the rich man left in indignation. Unfortunately, the rich man had to have anything that took his fancy. So one night he broke into the poor man's larder through the window, and stole the shell from him.

The night was dark, not a soul was anywhere, only the old cock was not asleep yet, and he saw his master quietly stealing back with the shell from his neighbour's.

Early the next day the rich man tested the magic power of the shell, and before lunch he had shaken it so many times that it yielded him three sacks of ducats. After lunch he set about shaking them out again, but this time all that came out was sand, and no ducats.

"Never mind," said the rich man. "I have got enough for today, and I shall go on tomorrow."

In the afternoon, the poor man came, and sadly asked the rich man whether he had happened to "borrow" his shell.

"How dare you, you cheeky beggar! Am I a thief in your eyes? Get out, before I throw you out!" shouted the fat man at his neighbour, and sent him packing.

The cock in the courtyard saw this. He crowed in a mighty voice:

> *"Cock-a-doodle doo!*
> *Do you know what is new?*
> *A rich man has robbed a poor,*
> *Taking his shell in the dark night.*
> *He is evil in God's sight."*

The rich man got red with rage and bade the groom catch the impertinent cock and throw him down the well. The groom did his master's bidding, thinking it would be a good riddance. But it was not.

The cock in the well drank up the water — it was a dry period, and the well was nearly dry, too — and in the morning, just as the servants were setting out for the fields and the courtyard was full of people, the cock flew out of the well, and sitting on its edge, sang out in a loud voice:

> *"Cock-a-doodle-doo!*
> *Do you know what is new?*
> *A rich man has robbed a poor,*
> *Taking his shell in the dark night.*
> *He is evil in God's sight."*

The rich farmer nearly had a stroke, he was so enraged.

At once he ordered the maid to catch the cock and throw him into the burning oven. And so she did. But there was a hitch!

The cock had his belly full of water from the well, so he put out the fire, and flew out up the chimney. He waited till noon when the courtyard was again crowded, then he took up his stand on the porch, and once again he struck up his throaty tune.

People came running together. Everybody was curious and the cock stalked about on the porch, and trumpeted his charge louder and louder. Of course, that was where he made a mistake. He ought to have been more careful.

All of a sudden, the rich man, all blue with rage, rushed out of the door, seized the cock, wrung his neck and threw him into the kitchen.

"Tomorrow I wish to have him for lunch with stuffing and raisins!" he ordered, and this came to pass.

He invited guests to attend his festive dinner, and they were all drinking, feasting, and indulging in foolish talk. They enjoyed the cock's meat; the host enjoyed it most of all, he even made loud smacking noises. Having finished, he wiped his greasy chin, and lifting a cup of wine, was about to propose a toast.

A hushed silence followed. However, the moment the rich man opened his mouth, the cock's head jumped out of it, and what they heard was not a toast but

the following words:

"Cock-a-doodle-doo!
Do you know what is new?
A rich man has robbed a poor.
Taking his shell in the dark night.
He is evil in God's sight."

The guests were flabbergasted. There was dead silence. The rich man shut his mouth. The cock's head disappeared in it. But no sooner did he wish to speak again than the cock re-emerged between his lips, and trumpeted the charge that the host was a thief.

The rich man saw that the cock would not leave him in peace until he had made amends for his evil deed.

So he called the poor man, begged his forgiveness in front of all his guests, and returned the stolen shell to him. It was no use to the rich man anyway. Even those three sacks of ducats had turned into sand in the meantime.

Afterwards things were once again as they had always been. The only difference was that the poor man was not quite so poor any longer, and the rich man, having disgraced himself so badly over the stolen shell, found that people avoided him. The cocks went on stalking proudly in the courtyard, keeping a watchful eye on people, and crowing their throaty cock-a-doodle-doos.

The Thief's Apprentice

Once upon a time, there were two brothers, but they were not at all alike; it was as if each were made of a different dough. The older one, a prudent farmer, had a good wife and three sons, and they all worked in harmony on the farm.

The younger one was something of a misfit. Farmer's work was not after his taste. He lived in a forest cave, and earned his living in a happy-go-lucky way, mostly by stealing. Sometimes he felt jealous of his elder brother and envied him his peaceful life. So he resolved to entice at least one of his nephews away from the farm, and teach the boy his unholy trade. That, he knew, would enrage his brother.

So one day he led the oldest of his brother's sons to a clearing in the forest. The young man looked around for a while, and then said:

"This will make a fine field when those stumps are dug up. Forest land is very fertile, uncle."

This lad will make a good farmer, he is no good for the thief's trade, the uncle decided, and sent his nephew home.

The next day, he brought the middle lad to the clearing. The latter looked round, again and again, until all at once his eyes sparkled, and he said pointing to a felled ash tree:

"Look, uncle, that is fine wood. Good for sledges or for wheels!"

"You, lad, are no good either for training as a thief," thought the uncle, "you talk like a would-be joiner or wheelwright."

The third day, he set out for the clearing with the youngest nephew. The boy had been a rogue from his very early days, his eyes were always full of mischief. He did not even look round a great deal. Right at the edge he caught sight of a curved hazel-nut tree, and he drew his uncle's attention to it:

"Crikey, that would do for a proper club! Swing it across somebody's back and he will laugh like hell!"

"You are right, my lad." And the uncle grinned contentedly. "You shall be my apprentice. Your father will stare to see what a devil of a boy I have made you grow into!"

And the youngest of the brothers became his own uncle's apprentice to learn the thief's trade. And he found the free and easy life in the thief's den in the middle of the forest quite pleasant.

One day the uncle said to his nephew, "Today I am going to show you how easy it is to steal a horse. Watch me carefully, so that you, too, may learn it." The boy was an observant apprentice, and always on the alert.

Towards evening, they walked to the forest path which led from the town, and hid in the undergrowth. After a while they could hear the clatter of a horse's hoofs, and in the bend a strange rider appeared — a thick-set parson in a black cowl. Suddenly, the curfew bell was heard from the nearby village. The parson dismounted, took out his breviary, and stepped out in a dignified manner along

the path, leading behind him his horse by the bridle, and softly mumbling his prayers.

That was the right moment for the uncle. "When I have unharnessed the horse, you shall throw this rope around his head, and lead him into our cave," he whispered and silently crept towards the horse. Taking away the saddle, he put it quickly on his own back; then he carefully took off the halter and bridle, and put them on his own head. At the same time, he nodded to his nephew, who quickly threw a rope around the horse's neck, and stealthily disappeared in the forest.

Meanwhile the uncle had bent forward to make the saddle sit more firmly on his back, and stamped the ground behind the pious parson, who was deeply immersed in his evening prayer, and had not an inkling of what was going on behind his back.

However, all things come to an end, and so the parson finished his prayers, shut his breviary, and turned round to mount his horse again. But seeing a bearded fellow on the bridle instead made his very blood curdle: he dropped his breviary, then quickly rubbed his eyes to make sure he was not seeing things. By then, however, the uncle had thrown himself on his knees before the astounded parson, and started off a long litany in a voice full of feeling:

"Your Reverence, my master, my benefactor, you are my generous deliverer. For seven years, seven months and thirteen days I was transformed into a horse by a magic spell. How many masters have I had, how hard they drove me, and how many whips they broke over my back! Until you, Your Reverence, took pity on me, fed me well and did not beat me, and your fervent prayer today finally delivered me from my animal form. To repay your goodness, my benefactor, I will never leave you. Until my dying day I am going to serve you like a real horse: you can put me to the waggon and to the plough. Jump up into the saddle, I will quickly take you home to the Rectory. You may use me entirely at your pleasure."

"Goodness me, what a predicament," mused the perplexed parson. "What shall I do with him now? I cannot feed him oats, and meat has become expensive. I would have to clothe him, too. He couldn't possibly go about in these rags. And to ride him like a horse? That's impossible. What would people say?"

So it did not take the parson long to come to a decision. With his face widening into a kind smile, he said in a gentle voice:

"I am really happy, my dear man, that thanks to my prayer the terrible enchantment was taken off you. Now you are free again, and why should you do the hard work of a horse? Go where your legs will take you, and remember this day with gratitude."

"This is a day I will never forget," professed the uncle eagerly. "But what about the saddle and the halter, Your Reverence? I will take them to the Rectory."

"What would I do with them now that I have no horse?" asked the parson. "Keep the saddle and halter as a reward for your faithful service."

In parting the uncle thanked the parson and bowed before him, but inwardly he laughed at his foolishness.

The evening in the robber's cave was a jolly one. The nephew had nothing but praise and admiration for his uncle's cleverness.

On the next market day, they sold the horse and the saddle to advantage, and were rolling in money.

But every pocket has its bottom. And so one day when they had changed the last coin, the uncle said:

"There is a market in the town tomorrow. We will lie in wait for someone who will be return'ng with what he has bought."

The next day, the two robbers were once again lying in wait by the forest path hidden in the undergrowth. And once again there was a sound of hoofs heard in the distance. This time, however, it was not a horse-rider but an elderly woman leading a cow who appeared in the bend.

"Even a cow will come in handy," whispered the uncle. "Now it's your turn. Do your best to get the beast by cunning and without violence; mark my words!"

The apprentice was neither a dunce nor a clumsy lout. Silently he ran ahead of the woman, and laid a glove across the path.

The woman walked with her head sunk low wondering how much milk the new cow was going to give, but suddenly she saw the glove on the road. For a second, a flame of cupidity appeared in her eyes, but presently went out again; what good would one glove be? And so she stepped over it, and walked on. After a while, beyond the bend, she saw another glove lying before her on the road.

"Well," she said to herself, "they will do for the winter!" She tied the cow to a birch, picked up the one glove, and quickly went back to fetch the other.

In the meantime, the lad had untied the cow, and disappearing in the brushwood took it straight to the cave.

The uncle praised his apprentice for having done a clean piece of work. They put the cow on a long rope so that it might graze behind the cave, and set about preparing their supper.

"What about a pot of fresh milk? That would be a bit of all right, man, wouldn't it?" said the uncle all of a sudden. "Take a pail and go and milk the cow!"

The boy went. Dusk had fallen in the wood. He found the cow, but, never having milked a cow before, he just could not do it. The animal knew this and was very restless. Every now and then the cow slapped the boy's face with her tail, every now and then she stepped on his bare foot with her hoof. Afterwards, she pressed him against a tree with her powerful back till he cried with pain. He beat her, groaned aloud, but all in vain. The cow did not give in even when, in tears, he cried and argued with her:

"Let me go, it's not my fault, I was not alone. It was the uncle who put me to it. So let me go, please, you'll smash all the bones in my body! I will be good from now on, I promise!"

The uncle heard him, and took fright. "We're in trouble," he said to himself, "the lad has been caught by the village beadle, who is thrashing him now. It does not surprise me that he has given everything away, and is putting the blame on me. Must be off quickly, or else I am sure to go before the court," he decided in a moment, and took to his heels. God knows where he went. He was never seen in those parts again.

The boy did not succeed in milking the cow. After a while he returned to the den — and found it empty. He called to his uncle, waited and waited, but in vain. So he went to sleep. In the morning he untied the cow, and took her to the village for which the woman had been heading. It was easy to find out where she lived. The whole village knew that the poor woman had lost her cow in the forest. He told them he had just found it and wanted to return it.

The woman thanked him with tears in her eyes: "I will be grateful to you, lad, as long as I live. I spent my last money to buy that cow, and my children would have had to go without milk. You are a good man, I can see it in your eyes. You are sure to make a success in life. You shall see."

And indeed, her words came true. The boy returned home to his father, and worked hard on his farm. He enjoyed the work, and did it well.

As to his apprentice years, he recalled them at times, but never spoke about them.

The Animals
and the Cottager

In the old days of legends and fairy tales both men and animals spoke the same language, and as they understood one another, there was no strife and quarrel among them for a long, long time. But man was always more ingenious than the animals. Though he was unable to fly like the birds, to swim under water for a long time like the fish, or to compete with the bear in strength, the other creatures gradually began to envy him.

What happened was that a small, almost pigmy fellow, built a cottage on the green by the forest; and this was not the end of his efforts. Before long, he had hens and ducks in his little courtyard, dainty morsels for the fox to long for. Then he led out to pasture a little flock of sheep, and these became the object of the wolf's desire. Finally, the cottager cleared and rooted up a piece of the wood, turned it into a little field and planted it with sugar beet.

Well, the sugar beet grew so big and sweet it made your mouth water. The bear stalked round it as if it were hot porridge.

He could not keep his paws off it for very long. One night when the cottager, tired after the day's toil, was sound asleep, the shaggy creature took over the husbandry of the field. He stuffed himself full, until, his belly swollen to bursting, he barely managed to roll away to his lair.

And while the bear was panting with delight the poor little cottager stared at the havoc and could not believe his own eyes. From the traces left behind he knew well who had been there, and he decided to punish the bear. He dragged a heavy log on to the field, and cut a deep, wedge-shaped crevice in it with his axe. Then he hid in the nearby undergrowth.

He did not have to wait long. The bear had become hungry during the day, and as soon as evening fell he hurried again to the sugar-beet field.

But alas! Even before reaching the first sweet morsel he felt his tail firmly clamped.

You see, in those days his tail was as hairy as the fox's, so it was caught in the log.

The cottager quickly drove the prepared wedge into the crack he had made, to prevent the shaggy beast from slipping away. At once he took a shaft and started beating the unbidden guest on his back, between his ears, on his paws.

The bear roared, whined, begged for mercy, but it seemed the cottager would never stop. Finally, in his despair the bear used all his strength and tore off most of his proud tail, for he was intent only on freeing himself from the log and the terrible shaft. Then he made off to the woods as fast as his paws would carry him.

He was moaning and groaning until he met the wolf.

"What has happened to you, godfather? And where is your beautiful tail?" the wolf was curious to know.

All the bear managed to say among his sobs was, "It's all the cottager's work .... he would have beaten me to death ..."

"The cottager?" said the wolf not believing his ears. "He dared do this to such a strong beast? Have no fear, I shall avenge you, and he'll never do anything like this again."

With these words he left the bear, and at once set out towards the cottage. Night had fallen, everything was dark and still, only the sheep were bleating in their sleep in the pen.

And that gave the wolf an idea: He pushed through into the pen, strangled the nearest sheep, and off he rushed with it back to the forest as if chased by the devil.

By that time the sheep in the pen made such a row that the cottager was up at once and hastened to them with the shaft in his hand.

He did not have to muse long to know what had happened. The bloody track still glistened in the light of the moon, and led into the woods.

"Just wait till tomorrow. Then we shall settle accounts!" cried the cottager waving the shaft. Full of anger, he banged the door, and then all was dark and still again.

The next day, the wolf stalked about the forest, boasting to everyone he met how he had avenged the bear, besides having a real feast himself.

"And tonight I'll go and fetch another sheep," he bragged.

This he said in front of the fox, who was herself after the cottager's hens and ducks, but being cleverer and more cautious than the wolf, she said to him:

"Well, well, I don't know, godfather. What will you do if the cottager sets a trap for you the way he did for the bear? Indeed, you haven't even so much strength as he has, to tear off your tail by yourself."

"Don't you worry. True, I am not so strong as the bear, but I can run faster. Besides, I would be sure to notice a log set as a trap!"

"Well, I only wanted to warn you, don't take it amiss," said the fox, and went her way.

So the wolf went on bragging to all the small animals in the forest, and when night fell, he set out again for the sheep pen, intent on his robbery.

He recalled what the fox had had to say, so he looked about him for anything like a beam or a log. But he saw nothing of the kind, so he ran as far as the sheep pen.

Just a single jump and he would be inside. But suddenly the ground under him gave way, and the wolf fell headlong into a deep pit which had been dug there and covered with loose sticks. He had not even time to scramble up on all fours, before the cottager was there, thrashing him from head to foot mercilessly till hairs were flying about.

He could have beaten him to death, the wolf was lying at the bottom like a carcass, and the blows were still coming down on him as though they would never stop. Finally, the cottager left off. He grabbed the wretched robber's fur with his firm hand, and throwing him out on the path, said to him:

"Be glad that you have escaped with your life. But I let you go only because I want you to give a message to everybody in the forest once and for all that anybody who comes here to do mischief shall not be spared!"

More dead than alive, the wolf came reeling back to his dwelling before daybreak, and who do you think he saw waiting for him there but the fox?

"You seem to be badly battered, dear godfather, what on earth has happened to you?"

"The cottager nearly killed me," whimpered the wolf. "He set a trap, a pit covered up with loose sticks, and then he took the shaft . . . believe me, fox, man is cleverer and stronger than we all are put together, we shall have to leave him alone."

Having said this, the wolf, all tired and aching, fell asleep like a log, and in vain did the fox try to make him tell her some more.

That man was strong, and that he was cleverer than the bear and the wolf, she readily acknowledged. But don't .ell her he would outstrip even her — the fox — in cleverness. Oh no!

This was something the fox could not accept, and she decided it was high time she went to the cottage herself.

It was broad daylight when she set out on her trip, with a willow switch in her mouth. She was in no hurry, did no stealing, and her ginger tail was there for everyone to behold.

The cottager was toiling in his tiny field. He saw the fox, and wondered why she was heading for his house. So he stopped working, seized the shaft which he carried about him at every step, and made for the unbidden guest.

He opened the gate, and stood dumbfounded: godmother fox stood in the middle of the yard, swishing her tail, and the terror-stricken ducks and hens were running for their lives in all directions.

"It's just as well you've come," the fox addressed the cottager. "For a long time now I've been wanting to tell you I will take those ducks of yours, at least for a while, down to the pond and for grazing. What miserable existence are they having here on this barren bit of ground?"

For a moment the cottager gaped at the fox like one entranced. He just could not understand how she had come to be so good-hearted. At last he muttered, "I see you have a swishy tail for the purpose. Well, just take them to the pond by the wood, but mind you are back before nightfall!"

"Why, of course, husbandman, you can rely on me," said the fox, and quickly set about driving the ducks out of the cou tyard, before the cottager should change his mind.

Anyone who saw the fox that day, driving a flock of ducks towards the pond, had to rub his eyes to make sure that he was not dreaming.

But it was no dream. Godmother fox was behaving like an experienced goose-girl, and it was only after they had reached the pond, and the cottager could see them no longer, that she told the ducks what she was really up to.

"There will be no bathing, I am going to eat you all up!"

The ducks were so terrified they did not even try to escape, but lay down in the grass half dead with fear. Only the old drake kept his head and said to the fox:

"Well, you have managed to outwit even the husbandman. From here we cannot call for him to come and help us. But have a little forbearance and allow us to sing a last song before we die."

"Just please yourself and sing," said the fox condescendingly, flattered by the way the drake had praised her cunning. "But whoever stops singing first will be the first to be eaten," she added severely.

The drake just nodded his head in agreement, made the whole flock sit in a circle around him, and the ducks burst out into such singing that before long the fox's head was tingling.

As you know, ducks cannot sing at all, and so they just gaggled together nicely in the circle without getting at all tired.

They might have gone on quacking like that to this day if it had not been for the cottager, who appeared on the path with the shaft in his hand. You may be sure the fox did not wait for him; she preferred to make herself scarce in the forest; and she swore she would be revenged on the drake one day.

The cottager was angry. The fox had not harmed any of the ducks by tearing out as much as a single little feather, but the man felt cross with himself for having let the fox beguile him.

And to this day people dislike the fox because of her cunning.

The Old Man's Advice

Far, far away in the north, where the summer is short, and the tiny fields so poor and stony that they hardly keep alive those who work them, there lived men whose hearts must have been made of stone as well.

In fact, in order to save food, they thought nothing of taking away on sledges old men no longer capable of lending a hand on the farms, deep into the forest, and leaving them there to be devoured by beasts of prey. Thus, instead of helping each other, and making life easier for one and all, men in the area were made heartless by want.

In one of the cottages there lived a very old man, who had a farming son and a lively grandson. In the spring of that year the farmer became well aware that try as he might his father could no longer hold the plough. Nor was the old man strong enough to tidy up the courtyard, or even to milk the cows; instead he was idling all day in the room by the warm oven.

"If you go on like this, I shall have to take you to the forest on the sledge when winter comes," the farmer said to the old man one day when he returned from the field to find that the old one had spent the whole day playing with his grandson.

The old man hung his head and whispered, "Perhaps you are right, I am no longer good for anything. Only allow me to take care of your son till winter comes. He is growing up untended when you are away at work all the time."

The farmer was dumbfounded by the answer. Why should anyone need to look after the child? But he nodded, and quickly left the room.

And so as summer drew to its close, the old man and the boy would go together to the forest, where the old man would point out to the boy the spots where mushrooms sporting hats as big as carriage wheels were to be found, and teach him to know birds after their voices and animals by the traces they left behind. In the brooks they would angle for crabs and fish, and before long the boy learned all about herbs, and how to cure the sick with them. On damp and chilly days when there was a nip in the air, he would listen to his grandfather's tales about faraway lands, famous battles and lovely princesses and gallant heroes.

But then the first snow fell, and the old man grew sad. He hardly said anything, and day in day out worked on making a sledge for the grandson. In the end it was much prettier than any other in the neighbourhood, and the boy was greatly taken with it.

When the frosts set in, the farmer put the poor old man on the new sledge to take him to the forest, to leave him there for good.

It was a sad journey, although the snow was glittering in the frosty sun, and the sledge was gliding swift and smooth like a feather. The two men did not exchange a single word, but the old one was secretly wiping away the tears that filled his eyes.

The father and son had no idea that they were being followed by the grandson. He had been struggling with the snowdrifts, and so he caught up with them at the very moment when the farmer was about to turn back without a single word of farewell, leaving the old one sitting powerless in the sledge in the middle of the forest.

"Why are you leaving Grandpa here on my sledge?" cried the grandson, panting for breath.

The father was more than put out by the boy's unexpected appearance.

"Everybody takes their old people to the forest when they can work no more. And the sledge is not worth much anyway," he said, embarrassed.

But the boy would not listen. "It is the best sledge I know. None of the boys has one like it! Anyway, if we leave it here now, what shall I put you on when I take you into the forest after you get old?"

At that moment the farmer realized the cruelty of what he was doing. He stroked the boy's hair, and said, "You are right, my boy, we mustn't leave Grandpa here. No matter how little we may have to live on, we will look after him. And you shall keep your pretty sledge."

And the husbandman kept his word. They all returned to the cottage in a happy mood, and chose to eat as little food as possible, rather than get rid of the old man.

The neighbours reproached the husbandman for what he had done.

"Just wait till there is a bad harvest! You'll all starve because you have one mouth more to feed!"

The farmer took no notice of their black prophecies. But the very next year there was such a severe drought that he harvested hardly a bushel of rye. He knew only too well they would find it hard just to live through the long winter, let alone keep some grain for seed. So he walked about like a lost soul, and kept out of the old man's sight till the old man himself stopped him one day saying:

"I know what is worrying you, my son, but may I give you a piece of good advice?"

"That's what I really could do with, but how can I expect help from one who no longer does a spot of work himself?" snapped the husbandman.

"Well, it's true I can't work any more," said the old man with a sad smile. But the next moment his face brightened up: "Do you see that roof on the barn? It is all made of thatches. Tear down one half of it, and give the straw a new threshing. Then do the same with the other half and you shall see . . ."

The farmer eyed the old man with distrust, but did exactly as he had bidden him. And lo! By threshing the thatches he obtained so much grain that he no longer had to fear starvation, and even had a whole bushel left for seed.

He was grateful to his father and looked after him even better than before. Moreover, when the good advice spread throughout the region and saved people's lives, the old man achieved what he had most fervently wished for.

From that time on old people were no longer taken to the forest to die. Instead, they were held in great esteem. And no wonder! An old man or woman is a storehouse of great riches, the bearer of wisdom and experience. And he is ready to share it with everyone else.

The End of the Tale
of Bird Bulbulis
and the Amber Ring

The last words died away, the birds' song sounded again from above, and Prince Ilin said, "Those were indeed lovely stories. I only wish my father and brothers had also heard them."

"You really have a good heart," said the Queen of the Seas. "They wanted to drown you, have you forgotten that?"

But Ilin answered:

"They are sure to feel sorry now. And I would particularly like for my father to hear these fairy tales."

"If you insist, we can return to your home tomorrow. But you must have a rest now. You may not have noticed, but you have been listening to the tales for a whole month!"

Ilin was happy to obey the Queen of the Seas. And while he slept, the sea-nymphs and fishes built a bridge of amber which led from the depths all the way to the royal castle.

At dawn a golden carriage and six horses were already waiting for the prince and the Queen of the Seas, and the horses drove over the golden bridge so quickly that Ilin's eyes were dazzled by the glitter he saw.

When they reached the familiar gate, it was really just in time. Bird Bulbulis was silent — just sitting and looking downcast in his golden cage, and the old king was nearly dying, he missed Ilin and the fairy tales so much. And the brothers? They were ashamed of what they had done to the youngest, and were afraid to confess their misdeed. No sooner had Ilin and the Queen of the Seas appeared in the doorway than they pressed him to their hearts with joy. Even the old king jumped out of bed, suddenly fit as a fiddle.

Thereupon Ilin put the amber ring round Bird Bulbulis' claw, and turned it round nine times. And once again, just as in the castle under the sea, Bulbulis' song sounded and then the enchanting fairy stories were told one after the other.

However, it was not only at the castle that people heard them. The king had all doors, windows and gates opened wide so that the fairy tales might fly to the four corners of the kingdom and everybody might hear them.

What more is there to say?

Well, only that Ilin forgave his brothers their evil deed, married the lovely Queen of the Seas, and when his old father died, became a wise ruler himself. Bird Bulbulis assisted him with his fairy tales. For it was enough to turn the amber ring nine times and ...